HEAVY
WEIGHT OF
DARKNESS

JM ERICKSON

OTHER WORKS BY J. M. ERICKSON

Action/Adventure Thrillers

Albatross: Birds of Flight — Book One

Raven: Birds of Flight — Book Two

Eagle: Birds of Flight — Book Three

Falcon: Birds of Flight — Book Four

Flight of the Black Swan

Science Fiction

Endless Fall of Night

Afterlife Code

Time Is for Dragonflies and Angels

The Prince: Lucifer's Origins

Future Prometheus: The Series

Intelligent Design: Revelations to Apocalypse

"... 'A house divided against itself cannot stand.' I believe this government cannot endure permanently half slave and half free. I do not expect the Union to be dissolved—I do not expect the house to fall—but I do expect it will cease to be divided. It will become all one thing or all the other. Either the opponents of slavery will arrest the further spread of it and place it where the public mind shall rest in the belief that it is in the course of ultimate extinction; or its advocates will push it forward till it shall become alike lawful in all the States, old as well as new, North as well as South ..."

—Abraham Lincoln, Republican State Convention, June 16, 1858

PART 1

"I'm not even in your fucking war anymore."

PROLOGUE

"MAGISTRATE, it's been four years since New Georgia fell. And I have not been anywhere near Mars to be held responsible for the two other colonies going dark. Maybe they are rebelling," said Willard Bennett, former captain of the *Jefferson Davis*.

The room itself was too large for eight people—three judges elevated above where a prisoner would stand and four armed guards, two flanking each side of Bennett's back, close enough to grab him but far enough to respond if attacked. Dim lighting, dark wood-like material absorbing the low light, no chairs but for the judges, and no spectator benches. He was sure the minimal lighting over the judges was to cast shadows, obscure expressions, and create mystery. This courtroom was for closed-session, high-security meetings. Bennett had been there before his last tour as captain of the *Jefferson Davis*, where his instructions were clear and to the point. He had come to understand that if he had followed orders and simply killed the prisoner he was transporting and made it look like an accident, he might have kept his commission, status, and ship. It took him six months of solitary confinement to come to that decision.

Greed and the opportunity to be rich had ruined him and killed his command staff. Hard lessons. It took an additional six months in the general prison population to own his role in his present situation, but he was not going to be held accountable for events occurring while he was en route back from Mars and in prison.

Honestly, how can it be all my fault what happened to them after? he thought.

"Not completely true. Your decision to disregard the original directives given to you in this very room may have set the stage for what happened," the older of the three military judges said.

Bennett was still standing, as was customary for a military prisoner in front of a review panel. In front of him was a table with three monitors showing security footage feeds from various locations of patricians being attacked, eviscerated, and dismembered by large dog- and catlike creatures. Other images showed half-dressed primitives carefully, methodically, and covertly breaking into storage and munitions stockades at various secured colonies, ushering slaves and plebs and anyone else along with them. He had seen these images before over the years and had come to hate them, especially the ones that showed his former chief medical officer tending to Black slaves, and even more, he hated a relatively small, athletic White woman with red hair leading the raids, whom he once knew as Cassandra.

"Are you paying attention, Convict?" another judge asked.

"Yes," Bennett said.

He was still not used to being spoken down to or his words being challenged. He had been interrupted, reprimanded, and put in isolation for disagreeing with any decisions these younger judges made. He continued to practice restraint. The bright-orange jumpsuit and limb- and throat-locking devices truly added to his fall from grace, with his uniform, property, riches, power, and position stripped upon his return to Earth two years ago. He was far thinner now, and he had to harden up and remember all the military fighting, training, and exercises he never thought he would actually have to use once he commanded his ship. In his time in prison, he'd had to live with slaves, plebs, and lesser humans. The poor food, lack of warm clothes and bedding, threats and acts of violence all the time, and no privacy anywhere—all of this was hell to him. He had been ill more times now than he had been in his life, and since his annual genetic dosages were no longer available to him, he would age and be susceptible to cancer, a disease effectively cured by patrician science for those patricians *in good standing*, which he was not. Still, it was being talked down to that bothered him the most.

"If you had managed your prisoner well, your command staff and guards might have lived. And if you had taken the time to launch a thorough investigation and destroyed those monsters and stopped those mutineers who assisted this Cassandra Kurtz, New Alabama and Mason Dixon might still be running, and New Georgia could have been rebuilt."

"I mean, if you had just killed that girl as originally ordered instead of being greedy, you might not be where you are," another judge added.

That statement hurt the most. *There is nothing worse than someone else pointing out a personal, massive mistake that can't be defended or denied,* Bennett thought. Not a day went by without recounting his errors and lack of judgment. Maybe this was the curse of imprisonment, to review all you did wrong and how it would have been simpler to stay on mission. Dumb.

The older judge continued as if he had not been interrupted at all.

"Now, I don't know if it was incompetence or poor

judgment, and you hoped all of this was going to blow over, but you have a chance to offset your failure and make things right."

Bennett looked up from the monitors, which were still displaying havoc, chaos, well-orchestrated raids, and a familiar face—Gavin, he remembered, whose image was now captured on security cameras. This betrayal had made his heart jump but hearing that he could somehow make his situation better caused him more dread than excitement.

He was afraid to talk, so he waited. It had taken him years to learn not to speak and wait for his betters to talk first.

"You left a total mess on Mars. We have no idea where this Cassandra Kurtz is or where she is getting her people, but it is evident that she is behind all these attacks that challenge the very foundation of our society and jeopardize our expansion on Mars. She has evaded, escaped, and at times destroyed any unified force against her, and after nearly four years of being unchecked, we must put an end to her," the older judge said.

"Yes, sir," Bennett said. He really had no idea where this was going. He had already lost everything, so he could at least listen.

"Officer," one of the judges said. "Play the transmissions we picked up from these terrorists."

Bennett had no idea what the judge was talking about. There was a blanket of silence until it was broken by a woman's voice, subdued anger behind the thoughts that were thought out and direct, leaving no mystery as to whom she was, what she wanted, and whom the enemy was. Everything had been visual up until that point, but now, in place of images the screen reflected audio waves, rising and falling with every word the woman said. Bennett sat in dissonance of this Cassandra who had been on his ship and the voice that speaking now.

The low male voice documenting the radio transmission source, time, and location highlighted Cassandra Kurtz's strong, unforgiving, and confident voice. Not rushed or particularly feminine but deliberate with smooth cadence and even tone. Somehow, the way she spoke was just as threatening, as frightening, as the message she conveyed.

Transmission frequency 145.100 Hz—New Alabama, All Citizens' Band

". . . how is that I bleed like you, eat like you, shit like you, fuck like you, and will die like you but lived a much better life than you? No disease. No sickness. No struggles. That's what it was like when I was one of them: a patrician, first citizen to stolen wealth from plebs, surfers, and slaves. All power. No accountability. I was no better than you . . . We know where you are. You are out of your element. This is our world. Can you find us? Do you dare? You lack conviction. You have no moral compass. This is why we will prevail while you fail."

Transmission frequency 412.289 Hz— Mason Dixon, Expedition Team Bravo Six, Forward Operations—Echo-Tango 12

". . . now. I am you. I am you, and we are here, living in the dark shadows of a black continent on a red planet. And above are they—our enslaved brothers and sisters. Above us, on the surface, are their slave owners. We must free the slaves and all who want to join, and we must kill any that get in our way . . . They are no better than us . . ."

Transmission frequency 412.338 Hz— Mason Dixon, Expedition Team Bravo Six, Forward Operations—Echo-Tango 12

". . . They are looking for us. Every step deeper into our home, they die. They're not strong. They are soft, comfortable, and weak. They started with twenty-three soldiers, and now they are down to four, the four horsemen. The rest have fled the horrors that are our home. Madness killed them. Weakness killed them. The heavy weight of darkness killed them. Every passing day they look for us, they lose more of themselves to terror . . . There is nothing here for you other than sheer terror and horror."

Whether it was staged or not, the silence felt heavy, but her voice still echoed in his head: the taunting judgment, her harsh conviction that she and the insurrectionists were far *more* while people like him—the judges, all patricians—were less than.

How the hell did this happen? What happened to her? he thought.

"This woman is a menace to our industry and expansion. She is costing us billions in lost revenue and profits, and word of her freeing the slaves and plebs has made it back here, causing more trouble on Earth. We are on the brink of an apocalypse now, every day she lives and transmits this shit," another judge said, pointing at him as if he were personally responsible.

There was a brief silence. Bennett wanted to make sure it was his time to speak.

"Yes, sir. Where do I fit in?" he asked.

The silence was deafening. Even with the shadows obscuring their faces, he knew that all three judges were staring at him. His stomach tightened, and his mouth and throat went dry. He ran a hundred ideas of what was coming next, the most likely of which he thought would be a public execution for everything that had gone wrong.

"You are reinstated as *acting* captain of a Plebian Auxiliary Corps task force to find this Kurtz woman; locate and destroy her base of operations; end her reign of terror; stop the loss of property, especially the slaves; and execute all former *Davis* crew, regardless of position and citizen status. Do not leave a stone upon a stone, *Acting Captain* Bennett."

Bennett froze in place. He recounted each word to make sure he was not hallucinating or dreaming. He had to clear his dry throat before he spoke.

"Sorry, but, um, are you sending me back to Mars to kill Kurtz and everyone, and if so, I'll get my life back?" he asked.

"You will get part of it back: full citizenship with medical benefits, captain rank but no ship, and you would be able to retire with an honorable discharge upon returning to Earth. Whatever property you reclaim will go to eliminating your prison term and filling your coffers, and while you will be on a short leash with the ship's captain and command crew, you'll be free from your cell. That's a rather good deal, considering we could go with someone else," the judge said.

It is a good deal, Bennett thought. *Almost too good to be true.* Why didn't they go with someone else? He wondered if it was a real deal or whether, if he did what he was told to do and completed the operations, he would have an "accident" like what was originally planned for Cassandra. He wondered if he should pass, spend his ten years in prison, and hope he wasn't killed by the other inmates or guards. By the time he would get back to Mars, six Earth years would have passed, and his targets might be dug in deeper, with better resources and positioning. The whole planet might have changed by then. Maybe none of his kind—first-class citizens, patricians—would even be left alive by then. His eyebrows furrowed at the new thought. No more partitions on the whole planet. None.

"Well, Bennett? Are you in or out?" the older judge asked.

His moment was up. He did his best to snap to attention, as if he was fully committed to the offer.

"Yes, sirs. Search, locate, and destroy the terrorists' base; terminate Cassandra Kurtz's command; locate and return all property, especially slaves; reestablish societal, political, and economic structures for the remaining colonies; rebuild the potentially lost locations; and return to Earth," Bennett said. He did his best to project authority in his prisoner's orange jumpsuit and limb and neck restraints. His response was precise, crisp, and delivered with command, just as he remembered from before his fall from grace.

"We need you to document both visually and by DNA, but preferably bring her body, or if it's easier, just bring her severed head back to be a lesson for all others who challenge our thinking to see," said the third judge, who had been silent throughout the proceedings.

"Her head, sir?" Bennett asked.

"Yes, Acting Captain. Terminate her command with extreme prejudice," the older judge said.

With a nod, Bennett agreed, and his limb and neck restraints fell right off, leaving his body feeling lighter. He felt his stomach settling and relaxing for the first time in years. And while he felt a wave of relief, he was surprised he did not feel anger or hatred toward his targets; rather, he felt excitement. He couldn't figure out why, but he embraced the offer to be an assassin with zeal, though he was not remotely positive he would carry out *all* his stated objectives.

"Uncertainty is good," Bennett said to himself.

"What did you say, Captain?" the judge asked.

"Nothing, sir. I will proceed," Bennett said.

CHAPTER ONE

THIS MIGHT HAVE BEEN A MISTAKE, Bennett thought.

With an average-size, single door in right in front of him, Bennett stood looking at the only entrance and exit through light gray mall wall that spanned well beyond one hundred feet from floor to ceiling. He was not alone. He had three guards around him. They were a concession he had to deal with to get to the Delta Exchange, which was looking empty,

What a waste of time, he thought.

He had only three days left of his last seven on Earth. He had spent much of the time eating the best food possible along with wine, drugs, and sex, all on the admiralty tab. Reinstated as Acting Captain did have its perks. The only downside was that there was no time to get life-extending procedures and anatomical and organ regeneration before his trip.

Something to do once I get back, he had often said.

Still with the rest of the evening and two days of having an exciting time until he left for the Manassas, he did get access to Cassandra's files. These were the closed files never seen in the hearing. He had asked to see all the material associated with the fall of this great curse, the bane of Earth's patrician class existence. He hated to admit it, but the first time he'd seen her, he had been shocked by how plain and unassuming she was. His time with her on the Jefferson Davis opened a box of curiosity as to how a patrician, full first-class citizen could plummet such great heights from one of the most prestigious families in the Third Republic.

When the box showed up late at night when he was waiting for an expensive plebian whore, he made the mistake of peeking and finding two sets of files: a smaller set to which the public had access, and a larger set from the investigation. Once he opened the larger set, he lost track of time, never got laid, and was not able to sleep until he sifted through the documents for nearly two days.

At first, he skipped over her earlier life, which noted antisocial, distant relationships with family and friends from eleven years old and on. The materials, documents, and things called books had sweeping names such as The Constitution, The Declaration of Independence, and The Universal Declaration of Human Rights with various years going way back to 1945, after the fall of the Third Reich, a primitive predecessor of their great Third Republic, which every practician knew as the first fall of world order, long before the Great Conflict of 2041.

He saw documents about the most maligned leaders of the misinformed in old US history, such as Abraham Lincoln, followed by Franklin D. Roosevelt, John F. Kennedy, and Barack Obama—all delusionally supported by the lower IQ, mixed racial masses; undocumented, illegal aliens from equatorial countries; and misled Caucasian leaders who should have known better. There were still more documents and entities he had never heard of such as the International Criminal Court from The Hague, Netherlands, and various documents on a massive subject called crimes against humanity.

There was so much. The depth, volume, and breadth of

the material in her possession was impressive, and it wasn't even all of it. Most of it she had given to the black market that liberated surfs, plebs, and slaves, other disrupters of a stable world government. Still, as much as there was to influence a young mind, poison it in effect, the material looked authentic, genuine, of a vastly different world gone by.

Bennett was still processing and thinking while walking around his grand full bedroom suite, with delivered food containers everywhere and his bed a mess of papers, pamphlets, files, and computer tablets of still more data about places, events, and freedoms he had never heard of before. Still, he wondered how she'd gotten on this track at such an early age. What happened that would push her down a rathole of well-fabricated data points, lies, and mistruths?

Bennett rummaged through the box of classified material again and found a psychological evaluation report that he hoped would give him some insight as to her mental illness. He had to believe that she was crazy, her life distorted with hallucination and delusions. So sad, he thought.

Her psych report and clinical evaluation did a great job explaining things: In addition to some neurological deficits and a tendency for depression, she had been lost for about thirty minutes at the Delta Exchange, once the biggest trading posts for oddities, rare things, finding workers and slaves. Since then, there had been others that had grown and developed such as the Tennessee Triangle and Maven of Mississippi. All higher tech with customer service that boasted a "fulfilling, immersive experience."

Huh, thirty minutes in that place, and she became a shit-ton bag of trouble, he thought.

Three hours later, under guard for "his protection," he now wondered if it had been a mistake to waste an hour with the admiralty to get permission to "get in her head." He still had two hours of transport with three guards to make sure he did not escape.

———————

Located at the far end of a massive mall, patrician citizens shopping, eating and wandering around, he was amazed by how busy the area was outside of a notoriously known access point for soldiers to find anything they wanted before leaving or upon returning from space or out on the surface.

The wall, an easy hundred feet, had no windows, which was unlike any mall he had experienced. They were typically thoroughly encased in transparent metal to see a massive landscape cast in a dark reddish hue.

"Problem, Captain Bennett?" the guard behind him said.

"No, it's just not what I expected. I mean, how many people have gone through the other side through this, well, small, unintrusive door?" he said.

"Many a drunken fool looking for a fight, easy money, drugs, sex, and slaves or whatever helps you get rid of stress," the guard to his right said.

"We can leave if you want or wait here? One of us could go in and get you what you want," the guard on the left offered.

"No. This is for observational purposes for Mars," Bennett said.

He moved ahead and opened the unlocked door. A guard stopped him from going through first and went ahead to check on things. Even before he could hear the guard inside give an all clear, the other guard gestured for him to enter.

Once inside, the space was twenty feet away from yet another identical wall that created a buffer between them. The reasons became obvious; there were smells that were being recycled through massive machines above them that easily took up fifty of the hundred feet. The heat and stink that managed to be trapped between the walls was stifling. There was humidity too, almost as if sweat and body odor hung in the air. There was a double door in front of them, an ample collection of air purifying masks, and a set of rules and disclaimers that required biometric signatures, both optic nerve and handprint.

"Sir, you'd better take one of these. It gets pretty raw in there," a guard offered. Bennett took it but told him he would put it on only if it got too bad.

"The subject I am studying was here at eleven years old for thirty minutes without a mask. I'm trying to see how that might affect her," Bennett explained.

"Poorly, I bet," said another guard.

You have no idea, Bennett thought.

It was extremely hard to hear with the machinery running above their heads, and while the smell was tolerable at the moment with filtration and a wall as a barrier, he was trying to brace himself to the full onslaught on his senses once the main doors to the exchange opened. He imagined that there might be a lot of people, maybe some bazaars, shops, and workers. He wanted to make it to the slave block as that was the place where the authorities found her.

———

With the final biometrics completed on the last guard, the double door sprung open, and a "WE COME" in orange came on. Initially confused, he realized either by design, mistake, vandalism, or error, the WELCOME sign was missing a letter. He was about to say something when the noise hit him, then the odor.

"What the hell?" Bennett said.

"It's always a shock when the doors open. The barriers and filters do a really decent job keeping everything here at bay," a guard said.

The Delta Exchange was full, almost compact with people. Many patrician men and some women, all wearing filtration masks, were walking in threes and more, talking, pointing, and looking as they strolled around. He was surprised by how casual they appeared unless they were approached by a surfer trying to show them some goods they got from the surface, outside the biosphere. Then they would push them away or look at what they had to offer.

Bennett felt his eyes water. He couldn't tell if the smell moved from his nose to his eyes, or if the place was just filled with too much dust, dirt, or odors. There was a sweet and a pungent smell rivaling each other for dominance. He could determine that some of it was human sweat, and a lot of it. There was the smell of feces and urine in the air, along with vomit. While not overwhelming, he wanted to run out of the place screaming. He was aware that he might be putting his mask on sooner than later.

As he walked, he felt eyes fall on him, mostly surfers who approached him to sell something, but the guards kept them away. There were plebs, but he was surprised it looked like women only, maybe mothers and their daughters shopping, but he couldn't get his head around why any mother, even a nonpatrician mother, would bring their daughter to a place like this, and they were also without a mask. No masks at all.

To his left were mobile selling carts. Behind them were walled-in stores, food and drinking establishments. Again, there were more patrician men than women there. He looked to his right and saw more of the same.

Moving was slow. There were a lot of people, not just strolling or milling around, some just standing. Watching. Once he figured he was getting closer to the slaving block mall, he noticed he smelled more human waste, though it was still outmatched by the sweat. He had reached a point where the odors were unbearable, and he put his mask on. It was amazing. Nothing but pure air. Not a hint of any foul stench that was making him want to throw up.

"It's much better with the mask," a guard said.

Bennett continued to look around and started to notice a girl as young as ten or just around pubescence following a patrician man with a leash around her neck. She didn't look frightened, like he imagined a little girl might feel. Her eyes fell ahead of her, following without a word, almost immune to the smell that he knew was getting worse the closer he got to the slaves' quarters. He looked around to see if there were any similar sights of girls being led away. Some wore leashes on their necks. Others had leashes on their wrists.

He saw more groupings: One group of patrician men had two young women in the same bondage as the first girl he saw. Each man had a leash to each girl. While they looked like they were smiling and engaging, it felt off, not genuine, more of an act. He looked beyond them and saw a young pleb man, maybe twelve, leashed to two mature patrician women. Like the young girl, he was without a mask, eyes straight ahead, emotionless, being led by each woman with their own leashes around his neck.

From his peripheral vision, he saw two forms—an adolescent girl and a young plebian woman old enough to be her mother—approaching the guard on his right. The guard stopped, listened, said, "No," and then motioned them away. Bennett looked at them as they retreated.

"What did they want?" Bennett asked.

"She offered you companionship from her, her daughter, or both. It's hard for them to make a living, but plebian women bring in a shit ton of money compared to their men in the service or trades," the guard explained.

Bennett took a moment to process what he had heard and seen. It all came together for him, and he came to a stop. Matched by the casual nature by which the guard spoke of the sex trafficking of children, he was feeling stupid he had not seen it earlier, ashamed that it was patricians, his people doing it, and that everyone seemed to see this as the normal social order.

But it is, dumbass. This is the normal social order, he thought.

"What the fuck," he said quietly.

"Something wrong?" one of his guards asked.

"I'm sorry, sir, did you want companionship from that woman and her daughter," the other guard said. He took out of his pocket a rolled-up leather leash, like the one he had seen used for the other sex trafficking, as if it were a writing instruments, a tablet, or a cannabis mint.

"No, no. It's all just a little much," Bennett said as he started moving again.

The guards were saying something, but he had trailed off in his own head. He wasn't listening but focused on the obscenities he was seeing.

"I'm sorry, Captain, but is this your first time here?" a guard said.

Bennett nodded and kept moving. He really didn't want to talk about the situation anymore. He was beginning to think how a young girl, eleven years old, would think of this place, think of herself. Think of her being a patrician. He walked in silence for minutes. How long it had been, he had no idea. He stopped abruptly when he bumped into a barrier that kept the public away from the slaves that were being traded, bought, and sold for the day.

A nagging thought was recycling through his head – if she was right about an amoral place like this, maybe the stuff she was reading was not delusional at all, but real?

He looked at a two-foot-tall block where a young woman, with Black skin, eyes, and hair, completely naked, was being displayed in front of mostly men, a few women, all identifiable as patrician class. Instead of leather leashes, this woman had thin, glowing hand, leg, and neck restraints keeping her bound. All the onlookers had their masks on, talking to each other, comparing notes and then offering either money or trade. He discovered that in addition to cleaning, this slave could gratify male and female sexual needs with zeal. Bennett looked into her eyes, and they did not reflect any expression of zeal, like the poor, leashed plebs he saw.

———

The young Black woman was sold outright to a young patrician couple and an older adolescent boy they had brought along with them.

A family outing? Really, he thought.

After the sale was completed, an exceptionally large Black man was brought out, adorned with the same restrains as the woman. He looked strong but also very docile, as if he were drugged. He looked tall and big and clearly had muscles. Bennett was struggling with trying to figure out what was off.

"This specimen can work along with your plebs to do the heavy stuff so your machines and higher value plebs don't get hurt," the auctioneer said.

"He has been scanned for health issues and is perfectly healthy post operation, and he should provide years of heavy lifting, carrying, and service without issue, and there is no fear of propagations or violence," he continued.

As if to demonstrate what he meant, the auctioneer took a step closer to the slave, released his arm restraints, and revealed the man's crotch area that at that point had been covered, revealing he had no penis or testicles.

There was a wave of audible approvals and appreciation from the crowd, and the bidding took off in a frenzied state.

"Okay. That's it for me," Bennett said to the guard beside him.

"Sir?" he asked.

"I've seen enough. I want to go back home. Thank you for your time and patience," Bennett said.

The guard looked surprised by the courtesy but acknowledged it and directed the others to lead the way. Leaving was the best thing he could do, except there were similar sights on the way back. He was only fifty-four years old, and he was feeling ashamed that he had been so naive and sheltered for so long. How could he not know about the Delta Exchange and other places like that were now brand-new, updated, and improved for the customer experience?

The travel back was silent. He was lost in his thoughts. He knew such places existed, but he had never visited. It was an underbelly of his society – ugly, harsh, brutal, and worst of all, unnecessary. As a ship's captain, he saw the sanitized view. As a lost little girl who witnessed this horror, it had to be life altering for Cassandra.

While he remembered everything about how he got to the Delta Exchange, he remembered nothing about getting back to his messy, disheveled suite.

Once the guards dropped him off, he found himself still agitated, ashamed, and angry, full of excess energy. Instead of drinking, or fucking or getting high, he decided to do something different. He looked at his mess and decided to clean up his entire living space, from toilet to bedroom. He deposited bags of garbage and the clothes he'd worn to the exchange outside for service until he decided that he could just as easily drop the material in the disposal chute himself.

Once he was feeling less angry, he collected, collated, and organized the material on Cassandra and placed it back in its original box, as if it had never been opened or read.

All throughout his waking hours he kept having the same thought – if she was right about that shit hole, which he could attest to, then why would she be so wrong about wanting to change it.

He contacted the captain of the Manassas but was switched to the XO. He was a pleasant young man who had to relay the "bad news" that he would be put in cryo-sleep three days after departure from Earth. It must have made the XO's day when he requested that he be prepped and placed in cryo-sleep for the eighteen-month journey to Mars upon his arrival, if possible.

Bennett was hopeful that he would spend more time asleep. Better to have that violent, snowstorm of cryo-sleep in his head than remembering all that he'd seen in one afternoon. It had taken him only an hour, roughly the same time as Cassandra, for him to want to escape.

Doesn't take a genius to see what changed her, he thought.

"She was just a child back then. It must have driven her crazy to see what was happening and pretend to go along after seeing that shit," Bennett said softly.

She's no child now, he thought.

He didn't like feeling shame and guilt. He really didn't like feeling as if he had been duped his whole life and an eleven year old girl figured it all out when he was a grown ass adult piecing it all together. He didn't like feeling stupid. And he didn't like the idea that he understood her. He could even understand why she did what she did. He was thinking about that for hours until he fell asleep. It was not restful, more tossing and turning with brief periods of insights assaulting like icy water when he woke. Cassandra's transmissions were also making sense. Her voice became more haunting. with hidden meanings now available to understand.

"All power. No accountability," she'd said. He kept thinking of other things throughout the night: She's a movement, not a person. She's an idea, not flesh and blood, not killable.

The next day he woke up early and left a message for the

XO, asking if he could leave sooner than the launch period. He said he'd be happy to go "right into freeze and stay out of your way." Fortunately, the commander agreed, and within eight hours, he was on a shuttle craft, heading to the refitted Manassas. Normally, he would have read everything about the ship, being a former captain himself. That's what he liked to do. Used to do. But his heart wasn't into it anymore. He wasn't feeling like a captain anymore. No interest in history, legacy, personal accomplishments, nothing.

He took a look at his classified file while en route to his ride. He reread his orders about track, find, and kill Kurtz to terminate her command, and all the other requirements.

A blue klaxon light filled the empty shuttle to let him know they were in the last approach to the ship. He reached over to the disposal incinerator, a military grade disposal box for classified missions, and dropped the entire file in it, including all the "helpful" data to find and kill her.

I've got enough information, he said to himself.

He leaned back and looked at the retreating star field as the gray sides of the ship took up the screen view.

"I'm not even in your fucking war anymore," Bennett said.

Finally, the star field was gone, and he felt the retractors catching the shuttle craft's hook to stop. Without any fanfare or another word, Bennett got up without any gear, uniform. or kit and exited onto the Manassas, ready to find Cassandra Kurtz. He wasn't sure if he was going to be able to find her, but if he did, it was clear in his mind that she would probably get to him before he got to her, and he was all right with that.

CHAPTER TWO

BENNETT ALWAYS SAW A WHITE, silent background when he was in cryo-sleep. It was a perpetual snowstorm, blowing violently, but it was always silent. No wind, no sound. The transition from being awake in a man-size tube and a sudden frost enveloping his eyesight and all his senses might have contributed to the snowfield experience. What always amazed him about cryo-sleep was the dilation of time. Usually, it felt as if he'd just climbed into the tube when it was time to get out. It reminded him of when he would receive some life-extending procedure that required anesthesia, and it went from prepped to done with no awareness of time passing.

This time though, the silent blizzard seemed to continue for a long time. It felt much longer than his past experiences, certainly not "I just got in here" at all. In addition, he felt tired, which was never the case.

Maybe I'm getting old. My treatments are all off, so maybe this is what the plebs and surfs go through when they're put into cryo-sleep, he thought.

But then, all the memories from his last days on Earth returned—the Delta Exchange, slave auction, the pleb sex trade. He had hoped the sleep would just erase them, but as he knew, the sleep was only a respite and not a permanent solution. Only time could help that.

An old memory from when he read the Bible came to mind – "For in much wisdom is much grief, and he that increaseth knowledge increaseth sorrow."

Fuck me, he thought. No escape.

With those thoughts came the physiological grogginess. Other than the absence of the silent white blizzard, Bennett's first sense was garbled voices. Both male voices. One spoke more than the other. One was closer, and the other might have been deeper. He couldn't understand what they were saying at all. He focused on his breathing as it felt hard to do. He saw shadows, felt heavy, tired, and he could smell only that antiseptic grape smell that was overwhelming. He wondered if he was dead. He'd read that the last thing people lose is their hearing when dying, though he understood leaving cryo-sleep was as if he were waking from the dead. The realization that he was exiting cryo-sleep meant he must have arrived on Mars. That thought alone made him feel better. Now oriented to time, place, and circumstance, the sense of panic, uncertainty, and feeling weighed down all subsided, albeit slowly. He decided to focus on listening. Bits and pieces started to make sense. He shifted to swallowing as his throat felt tight and raw, maybe a byproduct of being intubated at some point during his journey. He'd had that experience long ago when he was captain of the Jefferson Davis.

That was a billion years ago, he thought.

It was on the return home his cryo-tube had failed—not enough to kill him but enough to keep him awake for one month prior to his arrival home, a solid month to speculate how it would all go. His mind trailed off to that event, and he still thought it would have been better to have died in his sleep than the following shame to come.

Over two years of imprisonment, awful food, loss of longevity, elimination of rank status, and commission. And now, I'm heading back to the shit where it all went sideways. What could go wrong?

He felt his jawline and chest tighten. He could now discern mechanical beeping that increased in rhythm, followed by voice that was lower and almost seemed concerned. He felt his face warming, and he forced his eyes to open, pried them open by force alone, even though his sight was still blurry.

"Don't rush the process," a concerned voice said. It was an older voice and sounded, well, kind, similar to the voice his own doctor on the Jefferson Davis before the last mission. In light of what he knew now, he was embarrassed to remember what he'd said to that doctor:

Why are you such an asshole, Thomas? Who cares about this fallen patrician bitch when there is money to be made? Do you want to be poor all your life? We have an opportunity here.

Bennett knew that the good doctor had been ready to leave the service for years once the Davis started transporting slaves to Mars. Bennett clueing him in about transporting their last passenger, and the eventual nightmare, had been seemingly the last straw for their relationship.

"That's it, slow down and breathe," the voice said to him. While his vision improved, he could see light flashing in each eye, and then a warm hand touching his forehead, throat, ears, and back and front of his neck.

"I'm checking to see if there is anything out of place and any bruising. When you're more alert and ready, I'll be doing a thorough physical. Please nod if you understand," the voice asked.

It took a little effort, but Bennett nodded. True to his word, the doctor, or whom he assumed was a doctor, was careful and thorough as he did everything twice. As he did, he spoke in a calm, measured tone.

"Just to update you, all your vitals and systems are showing green. While you have experienced some weight loss and some muscle mass loss, you are doing surprisingly well."

Bennett felt his eyes blink more, and he croaked out his first sentence.

"What . . . how long?" he asked, confused. He'd boarded the midsize cruiser Manassas a mere eighteen months ago. He had been impressed by the size of the ship compared to his light cruiser, and the receiving officer on deck was nice enough, though he never did meet the commanding officer and command team before going into cryo-sleep, a byproduct of him wanting to escape Earth and his new knowledge. He was positive that the captain and his crew didn't want to deal with his failed captaincy and all the chaos he'd been blamed for on Mars and on Earth either.

His thoughts were interrupted by a new voice. The tone, cadence, and choice of words were soft but held authority. While not a baritone, the voice was deep, almost solid, with little inflection. Commanding but not imperial, something Bennett knew he'd struggled with for the longest time when he was XO and beyond.

"Captain Bennett, my name is Fleet Captain T. J. Jackson Taylor of the warship Robert E. Lee. There's no way to sugarcoat this, so I will say it right out."

It had to be obvious to anyone looking at Bennett that he was very confused. Even as his eyesight was slowing clearing, and his hearing was improving, he felt his heart rate and pulse picking up again.

"Except for you and fifteen other crew members of the Manassas, all hands were lost in what appears to be collision. While there's still an investigation continuing, the nature of your survival and the other crew members is unique because all survivors were in cryo-tubes near the galley as opposed to the medical bays," Captain Taylor said.

Bennett felt like a vise was gripping his chest. His jawline narrowed, and his breathing became shallow, as if gulping air. His ears felt hot. He could now feel sweat on his brow, and he was at a loss for words. To increase his anxiety further, there was more medical beeping and air rushing into his face, cooling him down.

"Captain Bennett, please try to relax. Rest assured, you are safe now. I will have more answers for you later, but for now, I want you to focus on rest," the doctor said.

"Yes, Doctor Abbott is correct. I need you to focus on recovery, so we can solve this mystery," the captain said.

Bennett felt his head shaking side to side to indicate he was not done.

"Do you have something? Were you awake when this happened?" the captain asked.

"No," Bennett whispered. "How long have I've been out?"

There was a discernable silence, and a brief back and forth between the two men standing above him until the doctor answered.

"The flight log, black box, and cryo-tubes indicate you have been in limbo for three years, four months, and ten days."

He heard no more words after that. He felt his head lighten, and his body fell limp. If he had been standing, he would have fallen over. His vision faded to black, and it felt as if he had finally fallen into a deep sleep where instead of silent snowstorm whirling around him, he saw nothing but black.

CHAPTER THREE

"UNDER NORMAL CIRCUMSTANCES, I could have told many a tall tale about my time on the Jefferson Davis, but both time and tide wait for no man, and I have missed both," Bennett said.

Captain Taylor and Doctor Douglas Abbott smiled at his response to telling them all a story at the captain's table, the custom of any captain, present or retired, of a military vessel: to tell a story or two about travels, places, conquests, and adventures. But in addition to feeling weak from lack of movement and living in a tube for more than three years, his once-heavy frame felt more like a burden to support, even when sitting down. He could barely touch the food in front of him; his thin fingers were barely able to balance the fork and knife. The energy output required to chew, swallow, and seemingly digest what was in front of him also seemed impossible. In addition to losing thirty pounds, his sense of taste was profoundly reduced as was his sense of smell, other than detecting strong antiseptic.

It had taken him seven days to make it out of sick bay, and it was all about physical rehabilitation and physical therapy. The first time he saw his face and body in the mirror, he stood still, a mere shadow of his former self. Being incarcerated while on Earth did not help him either physically or mentally, but it kept him from indulging in wine, women, and distractions he had planned to have after his fateful journey. Still, losing his patrician status and the medical benefits for health and longevity had taken their toll on Earth.

The last seven days of liberty before launch, he'd had three and a half days of debauchery, and then truth laid waste over everything else.

More than three years in cryo-sleep took what was left. The image looking back at him was smaller in width and in height. He once was more than two hundred and twenty pounds and six feet two inches tall; now, he could see he'd lost thirty pounds and three or four inches. His thin hair, once dark and full, that had transitioned to peppered black and gray in prison was nothing more than strands sitting on his head like a worn-out bird nest. His healthy sheen of tight skin was now pale white, sagging in all the wrong places, and the wrinkles made for a topical map of years, showing wear and tear on his face. He had no idea how long he'd looked at himself, but the doctor guided him away and then ordered the staff to remove all other mirrors. It was the greatest act of kindness he had ever experienced.

The week of keeping away from the crew was a blessing, and Bennett did not need doctor's or captain's orders to stay put, recover, rebuild, and catch up on the last three years of turmoil. He would have stayed in sick bay until he had to go planet-side weeks later, but Captain Taylor's chat with him yesterday convinced him to come to dinner with his command crew. The chat was simple: "You can decline and stay here until we send you down to the surface, but it would be helpful to me if you came to dinner. Apart from my XO and the majority of patrician officers, the doctor and I and most of the crew need you to stand tall and firm."

Bennett's look of confusion was clear as the captain continued.

"First Officer Robert Lee VI and crew did not take well to my commission to a ship that he feels is his birthright, and he struggles with his emotions getting in the way of the mission. He and others blame you and the Davis for Cassandra Kurtz, while the doctor, engineer, surfs, and plebians and saw this coming years before the name Kurtz was ever mentioned. A blind man could have seen this tsunami coming."

The captain's talk had been the best thing he had heard in years—literally, in his case. The haunting memories from the Delta Exchange, feeling naive, duped, stupid, and defeated, wore heavily on him. And now to find like-minded people who saw the patrician class and authority as something that was crumbling, doomed to fall, made him feel less alone.

It was a lot to digest then as it was when XO Lee did not accept his declining to tell a tall tale. The younger man's chiseled jawline tightened, and small, piercing blue eyes stared right through Bennett, as if he were a mere apparition. The smooth skin of callow youth and thick blond hair without a strand out of place would have been perfectly cast as Bennett's foil if life were a stage and all were characters.

"Well, then, maybe not a tall tale, but how about your last mission?" the XO said.

What was originally a warm room with low, friendly conversation now flashed cold. For the first time in a while, Bennett felt his blood beginning to boil, vastly different from the past week of feeling old, defeated, and bitter.

"That's classified, son, just like my present mission is today," Bennett said.

He did his best to remain cool and unconcerned. He even

took a bite of mashed potatoes to demonstrate some kind of nonchalance. It didn't work.

"I'm the son of Robert Lee V. But you're right, Acting Captain. I should have focused on the public hearings, the ones where you let that bitch slip right through your fingers and who now costs our patriarch's purity so much damage," Lee said.

"That's enough, XO. Ask your question without being insulting. Part of our heritage is to be respectful to dinner guests, something your father was well known for," Taylor said.

Taylor's distinction between the XO and his father was not lost on anyone at the table. The XO slowly stood up, as did the captain. The threat of violence, a duel for honor, was mere seconds away from happening. Bennett had seen this once before in a twenty-eight-year career, and that was because the combatants were two drunk officers who missed every opportunity for promotion and blamed each other.

This was different. This was war. Bennett had seconds to respond, and he was surprised by what came out of his mouth.

"The young XO is right, Fleet Captain Taylor, about the trial and this Cassanda Kurtz. And I should not have called him son. I am not worthy, and for that, I apologize."

Everything—movements, sounds, air—all seemed stuck in amber. It was only the captain's and XO's slowly sitting down that brought life back into real time. There was the shifting of seats returning to place, a cough, and two audible sounds of drinking something, whether it was water or alcohol Bennett could only guess.

"To be blunt, as captain of the Jefferson Davis, I was solely responsible for that debacle. And if there was ever a flash point of a shifting, dangerous headwind assaulting our way of life, Cassandra Kurtz is the tip of the spear. I lost everything—crew, officers, commission, status, all of it—and this is my last chance, my only chance, to make it right," Bennett said.

"And your intentions are, Acting Captain Bennett?" the XO said, with enmity and doubt clearly evident on his face and in his tone.

Bennett took a moment to articulate what he had been thinking for years if he'd ever had a chance to do things again. And then he remembered seeing what an eleven-year-old girl saw at the Delta Exchange. He then decided to pull a couple of lines from his classified mission report.

That should do for now, he thought.

"I hope, with your help, to track her, find her, and kill her. To end this wasteful loss of life and enterprise. To preserve our way of life. And if not, to die trying."

While the tension and risk of violence greatly reduced, the air was still. It was clear that that someone had to say something. Finally, it was Chief Engineer Samuel Cooper who stood up with glass in hand to give a toast.

"To right the wrongs, make amends; rest in peace and no longer offend," he said.

Bennett found himself thinking it was an odd toast, though he appreciated the effort to get things back from spilling blood to eating dessert. The doctor and all the other officers at the table raised their glasses, pounded their hands on the table to support the sentiment. Bennett did too, as did the captain. The XO picked up his glass finally, but it was more to take a drink than it was to cheer.

Bennett watched the conversation and some positive emotions ebb slowly back into the room. The doctor and the engineer took the lead in moving things to a less-tense place, in addition to the XO's fraction. Still, Bennett could see that Fleet Captain Taylor and XO Robert Lee VI were periodically looking at each other, jaws clenched, nostrils still flaring, and shoulders still squared back.

This shit is going to go sideways real soon, Bennett thought.

Dessert arrived. It looked like a blueberry cobbler, still warm and aggressively melting the ice cream on top. Two bites, and Bennett was done. No taste or smell, and the fork was feeling too heavy to navigate.

Yup, this really does suck.

PART 2

No discernable expression on her face, she expressed a sense of stoicism, a calm in the face of strong headwinds, with an undercurrent of implacability.

CHAPTER FOUR

THE ONLY UPSIDE to being revived four weeks before arriving on Mars was being able to spend more time getting into shape. Narrow corridors and congested common spaces, cramped settings with three hundred men on board also allowed him to dodge, parry, and walk the warship *Robert E. Lee* many times and miles over and meet many of the crew. The forensic evaluations of the black box buoy transmission reports from the *Manassas* were close to completion while the debris fields revealed another set of information under analysis. The *Lee* had two escort ships, the *Virgina* and *Raleigh*, scouting out the drop zone for their insertion. This made Bennett feel much better.

As of late, he was less fatigued and could move faster. With the absence of significant weight and the additions of protein supplements and resistance training, he was feeling better than he could have imagined. Still, his senses of smell and taste remained diminished, and he looked much older than he should have. He shaved his head and wore military battle dress with no rank or insignia, all of which made him appear to most as a civilian hitching a ride from a military envoy. What surprised him most were the casual smiles from the crew. He felt a bit more optimistic, and most of all, he was not missing the military command rank, privilege, and responsibilities.

You know, this military contractor position does feel good. Maybe it's time to drop the "acting" captain title finally, he thought.

Captain Taylor and the command crew didn't seem bothered by his dropping the uniform and his puttering around the ship. His escorts did an excellent job remaining invisible, and there were times he thought he had lost them, but then they would be right beside him or in front of him, especially when he would get lost, which was easy to do on such a big ship.

Bennett also pondered why there were no slaves on the *Lee.* He had come to think that they were not skilled enough to be entrusted with such high-end technology until the doctor explained that the captain had removed all slaves, including the sex slaves, from all of his command ships, much to the anger and chagrin of his XO and his team. Much to the captain's disappointment, the escort ships remained heavy with slaves and then plebs while patricians numbered a mere dozen officers.

"The captain wants all crew members to be focused on the mission, and all motivated for success. Slaves have nothing to lose and more to gain if they are unsuccessful. Plebs and surfers have a lot to gain and more invested," the doctor told him.

"So, if there were a mutiny, unless the plebs sided with the officers, the officers are screwed, right?" Bennett said.

"Yes," the doctor confirmed.

The doctor also added in hushed tone, "And the captain does not believe in the slavery institution. His close friends and allies do not have any. A quality I like."

Bennett thought a lot about the captain, the doctor, the engineer, the XO, and the others.

I had three slaves of my own when I was captain and didn't have a problem with it, he remembered.

Now? After gaining some insight and being on a ship with most of the command crew and the fleet captain having none of the slave industry, Bennett felt shame from the past but hope for the future. A future he could consider. It was as if slavery was not allowed, and people simply didn't like it, or at least did not want to be around it. Further, this captain was obviously willing to fight when engaged, and Bennett found that he trusted him and followed his lead without even knowing why. Most of all, he had no envy or animosity toward the captain. He had often been prickly and angry at others who spoke ill of slavery, its usefulness, and how it didn't provide a better life for people. Now, he felt bad that he'd had slaves and wasn't angry at the guy who obviously did not care for this at all.

Maybe it's an age thing, or awareness that I'll die before I get my life back. Maybe I'm tired of the fight, he thought.

With just hours to go before the mission launch, Bennett walked toward where there were fewer crew members, and the reverberations from the ship's engines grew stronger. He was in deep thought when the XO pushed by him holding a bloody nose, and two of his subordinates were hot on his heels. The XO looked so enraged and pissed, he was not aware that he was banging into anyone who did not move quickly enough out of his path. Bennett felt his blood boil again and would have said something, but Chief Engineer Cooper poked his head out the engine room hatchway and yelled after the enraged commander.

"And if you have a problem with one of my crew members, come and see me, or you'll bang into another *hatchway* again!"

Bennett took a step back and alternated his gaze between the XO and entourage's retreat and the visibly pissed chief. The chief's face looked like the setting hot sun during an American West Coast summer. He looked back at the XO, who gave the chief the middle finger and never looked back. Before Bennett could ask what had happened, the chief saw him and motioned for him to follow. Without a word, he followed, not entirely wanting to find out what had transpired.

Well, maybe about an hour before the mission, and these two are fighting. What the fuck is wrong with these people? he thought.

The engine room was midship with the turbines, with engines and environmental controls making up the last half of the ship. Only the engineers and technicians cohabitated in this area while everyone else was midship to the ship's bow. How these guys managed to think and sleep with all the noise and vibrations was beyond him.

The short corridor opened into a massive cavern of machinery, computer servers, and equipment. There was one pleb being helped from the floor by two others, and another surfer was bringing the medic kit. Two other surfers were bringing a cot and liquids. It was easy to see that either the injured pleb started a fight with the XO and got the bloody nose, or the XO and his subordinates, who were disheveled but not injured, had started something.

"He's such a whining dick! You don't come into my shop and fuck with my people and expect to walk out whole! Fucking prick," Cooper said. He was now helping the injured man onto the cot while the others tended to him. There were two others that looked like they too got into a scuffle.

After a few minutes, Bennett risked speaking.

"So, is it normal for an XO to get a bloody nose? Was he implementing discipline?"

"No, sir," one of the surfers said. "Ellis didn't move out of the XO's path fast enough, so the XO started hitting him while the other officers started hitting us. It was the chief that broke up the fights."

"And who hit the XO?" Bennett asked.

"I did," said a surfer who was five inches and thirty pounds lighter than the XO.

"Shut up, Roberts! You know I did. Why are you always trying to get credit for fights you were never in?" a plebian said immediately. This man was even less likely to have done anyone any damage.

"Stop it, boys. I fucked him up, and if anyone of you tries to cover, I'll tell the captain and have you transferred to Earth," the chief said.

Silence filled the cavern, and every beep, motor, and electrical hum could be heard. The entire crew looked down.

I guess going to Earth is less than ideal, Bennett figured out. Earth was awash in one environmental disaster after another, but even in his brief transit from Earth to the orbiter, either his time away had reset his idea of what was bad, or things had gotten really bad while he was incarcerated.

"No, seriously, boys. I don't need protection, and don't put yourselves in harm's way. Assholes like the XO will make your life miserable for no reason at all, so don't give them any reason to bust your balls," the chief said in a soft, firm tone.

"Chief! Captain wants you to find Captain Bennett and head to the briefing room. He says we're green to go in two hours," another pleb yelled out from a small booth.

All eyes turned on the chief, who slowly stood up from looking at Ellis and was now eye level with his engineering crew.

"Thank you, boys, for your service and support. All shifts report in. I want you to focus on landing crafts, hydration units, O_2 scrubbers, and CO_2 converters. If we're going where I think we're going, the insertion teams will be underground, so air, light, and water will be critical. Also, pack compact sleeping kits with emergency blankets; they might be necessary for extreme climates, even if they are underground. And Connor—create a sleeping and break schedule for crew to have four six-hour shifts on the line while the mission is a go. We good, boys?"

A loud response of near-enthusiastic yelping and confirmation went up in the air. The chief pulled Ellis up from the cot with his newly fitted wrist brace and ice pack for his eye. For a guy that had been picked on, he was looking in great spirits.

"Good. I'll be back soon. Get shit done," Cooper said.

More cheers went up as Cooper waved Bennett to come with him to see the captain. It was only when the chief shut the engineer room's main hatch that the cheers from the engineers subsided.

As both Cooper and Bennett started the long walk back to the conference room, Bennett thought he would get some intel on what happened.

"So, the XO comes in and pushes your crew around. Gets physical, and you get physical back, and that's it?"

"Yup. The XO won't say anything because he doesn't want to be embarrassed, and he won't say anything to the captain because he knows that captain does not like punishing crew for punishment's sake. Discipline? Yes. But he knows the XO is an ass, and the XO knows the captain will be pissed and side with me and the crew," the chief said.

Bennett let the silence sit between them for about a minute before he spoke again.

"So, in addition to protecting your crew, you got a pass to pop the XO and rough him up and his team without real risk of punishment."

"Yup," Cooper said. "Unless something happens to you or the captain, I'll be safe, Acting Captain."

"This is true," Bennett said.

As the time passed, Bennett focused on the last thing the chief said. He wanted to ask the chief but kept his thoughts to himself

Now, is something going to happen to the captain? Me? My luck is sure to run out, but the captain? Shit, Bennett thought.

CHAPTER FIVE

"WELL, it's a good thing *I'm* the fleet captain, and you're not. So, stand down, take your seat, and let Specialist Betsy Ann Hall speak," Captain Taylor said.

"But, but, sir," the XO started, but halted as soon as Taylor held up his hand to stop him.

Without another word, the XO sat down at the other end of the conference room table.

"There's a reason why I did not inform you and others of Specialist Hall's presence. She is part of my revived military program called Military Assistance Command–Studies and Observations Group, or MAC–SOG. Not only is this program and her status need to know, which the whole damn ship did not, but I didn't want this expected distraction to limit our chance for success because of your opinions. So, while you won't find slaves on *my* vessel, you will find competent women, regardless of status. And even if she was a fucking slave with her experiences and insights, you'd be listening like you are now. Am I clear?"

Half the room gave an enthusiastic affirmative while the other half looked down and nodded.

Wow! This is going to be something.

While Bennett agreed that competence over status was important, he would not have sprung this on the crew minutes before a drop. But then, there was probably no time that would have been good. Any time before this, there might have been a mutiny, an assassination attempt, or overall, just a miserable ship.

"Specialist Hall, go ahead. Start with the black box transmission from the *Manassas* and what was discovered in the wreckage and debris field," Captain Taylor said.

An average-looking woman of mixed descent in her mid-twenties stood up and walked to the podium behind the captain's right side. She was athletic, with dark features and short hair. Two things stood out to Bennett: She had a prosthetic left leg, and she had a lifetime of creases and lines on her face from either ultraviolent light, stress or both. He could tell she'd spent time out on the planet's surface. Without seeing her hands, he was positive they had more calluses than he'd ever had. Her entire presentation spoke of experiences most in the room never endured.

Even with no discernable expression on her face, she expressed a sense of stoicism, a calm in the face of strong headwinds, with an undercurrent of implacability. She had seen much worse in her life than a room of older, angry, and entitled patricians who felt she had no business being there, telling them anything.

This is going to be interesting, he thought.

As she put her tablet down, a large screen dropped behind her, and all the conference table's screens lit up. An image of a human skull with a military beret appeared on a black background, with a gold border and lightning bolts with red initials spelling MAC–SOG. The image and this group were reminiscent of something he remembered from the academy decades ago, but his memory was unable to be more specific. Forgetfulness was a major side effect of discontinued age-extension procedures.

Getting old sucks.

"I will begin with *Manassas'* transmission and data logs, then proceed to the wreckage and debris field report and surface intelligence of the insertion team."

Hmm. Not bad. Clear, precise, orderly. Taylor might be right again. Good, strong voice too, Bennett thought.

"The black box transmission was significantly damaged. We found three useful messages that involved the wreck. One transmission command received earlier confirms that there were no anomalies: no human, computer, or mechanical problems throughout her entire voyage until she was in her braking burn for entering Mars's orbit," she said.

The internal ship recording on the bridge kicked on.

Bridge Day Report—13; Day 171, 09:45:04 Hours

"So, which is it, Comms: Are the scopes clear, or do we have a problem?"

"That was Captain William Anderson's first clear message," Hall said.

Bennett thought his voice was pleasant, undisturbed, and calm. The next transmission was noisy; sirens, warnings, yells, small bursts, and the popping of electrical arcs and panels breaking. While chaos reigned in the background, a young but steady voice could be heard giving a sitrep update.

Bridge Day Report—13; Day 171, 09:48:33 Hours

"Captain! A schooner identified itself as Clotilda, *captained by Robert Small. We have no record of him. She hit us midships from below. Took out the engine room and all aft . . . they came right when we were in burn and . . . rammed . . . why our engines exploded and went offline. Exiting crew from lifeboats confirmed unidentified boarding craft, no registry numbers . . . all navigation . . . we're adrift . . ."*

"That was XO John Mosby's report," Hall said.

Bridge Day Report—13; Day 171, 09:59:12 Hours

". . . we're locked on the bridge. We were boarded ten minutes

ago. The captain is dead, and the XO and Second Officer are engaging the intruders. Alex is directing the survivors away from the conflict to get them up here or to any remaining lifeboats . . ."

That voice was like the XO: urgent but well trained.

"And that was Lieutenant Nelson Pendleton, ship's navigator," Hall said.

There was an audible click, indicating that the report from the bridge was done. The lights dimmed, and the screen and tablets came to life. Aft visuals showed an engine glowing bright yellow and red. All seemed well until a shaft of brilliant light emerged from below the ship; the engines' braking system failed, and multiple arcs and explosions erupted from the midship going aft.

"This is the *Manassas* while it was in a braking burn maneuver. As you can see, the point of contact is oriented from beneath the ship. This is where the scope mentioned earlier must have detected something. While we have no visuals, we do have readings throughout the ship at point of contact, and it appears that she was hit by a civilian yacht, approximately seven percent the mass and volume of the ship. And while the *Manassas'* hull and reinforcement girders would have absorbed the damage, the collision was then followed by a massive explosion five seconds after impact. In other words, it was the timing of the collision that was critical, not the mass," Hall explained.

"Holy fuck. Captain, that schooner rammed her, then blew up its payload. What bastards," Cooper said.

"Agreed," Taylor said.

"The wreckage not destroyed in the collision and initial explosion show evidence of landing crafts blowing all ports open, and then the lifeboat ports were engaged," Hall said.

"And you know this how?" the XO asked.

The skepticism was evident as was his anger about a sister ship being destroyed.

"The ports show blasts blown inward toward the ship,

and the other landing craft show tether markings on the lifeboats. Further investigations show the *Manassas'* captain and defending crew used pulse rifles such as energy weapons and lasers while the attackers used gunpowder-propelled bullets from firearms: 10mm, 7.62- and 5.56-caliber," she said.

"Shit! Well-armed with primitive though effective weapons, an orchestrated ship attack from without and boarding craft and troops from within . . ." Taylor started.

He stopped and clicked on the intercom to the bridge officer on shift.

"Johnson here," a youthful, proud voice said.

"Johnson, sound yellow alert—have all crew combat ready, including sidearms. Once all crew is in place, lock down all ship compartments for potential depressurization. Alert the *Raleigh* and *Virgina* to follow suit," the captain ordered.

There was silence. Taylor looked at the intercom as if it could tell him what was going on before the voice returned.

"Ah, sir? Are we under attack? What did you want to do?" Johnson asked.

Taylor looked down at the intercom, closed his eyes, and sighed. Before he could act, another voice came on.

"Lieutenant Evans here, sir. Yellow alert, lock the ship down, distribute sidearms, alert the escorts. Aye, Captain. Do you want to launch combat shuttles? Three could easily cover the ship with overlapping paths."

Thank God! Bennett thought.

"Good idea, Evans—load three to circle the *Lee* and move scopes to focus for objects within a mile of our ship," Taylor said.

"Aye, Captain—three fighters and scopes for close inspections and potential collisions. Will transmit to *Raleigh* and *Virgina*."

"Thank you, Evans," Taylor said.

"Certainly, sir," Evans

The XO then tripped on his own intercom to speak.

"Lieutenant Evans, could you have Lieutenant Virgil Johnson meet me in my office for some words?" Lee said.

"Yes, sir," Evans said.

Taylor gave an approving nod to Lee, who did the same in return. A yellow klaxon flashed near the hatchway, a clear indication that crew and ship needed to be prepared for anything.

Well, nice to know you both see and deal with incompetence.

Bennett was about to think about what he would do when Specialist Hall started her report again.

"It also seems clear that whoever boarded the ship took their time and took various components ranging from wiring to computers parts, whole mechanical and electrical systems, and whatever was being hauled in the sealed compartment that was also blown inward," she said.

"Wait, that would have to have taken hours," the doctor said.

"This isn't a smash-and-grab. This was well planned," the XO added.

"They would have needed time, ships, and bodies to do all that," the captain said.

"Yes, sir. We think they had all three. All the lifeboats are missing, and except for two that landed near the garrison, Fort Sumter, the other twelve are gone. Their automated SOS was never initiated," Hall said.

"Fuck me," Bennett said out load. It was an unfiltered inner thought that bolted out of his head.

"Captain Bennett? Something to add?" Taylor asked.

Bennett cleared his throat. It was still dry from the cryo-sleep weeks ago, but it was far clearer and stronger than it had been.

"Specialist Hall, do you think that the boarders killed the

crew, used the slaves to take apart everything, and used the lifeboats to take it all away?"

"Yes, except to add that the slaves went with them," she said.

There was an audible gasp. Eyes shifted from one to the other. The full weight of what had happened to the *Manassas* was becoming clear. Captain Taylor's not having slaves on board was either fortuitous or tactical genius.

"What the fuck," Lee said.

Hall continued above the exasperation, surprise, and anger brewing as the cold realization of an attack, mutiny, slave uprising, and hijacking spread.

"While there are bodies of crew members, there are no slaves or any other crew members except patrician. There were some plebs and surfers near the impact zone, but the absence of slaves and other nonpatrician bodies implies that a relatively small boarding party could have breached the ship, freed the slaves and anyone else, killed the patrician crew, and had both the personnel and ships to strip the important parts of the *Manassas* and flee with minimal effort and time," Hall said.

More side talk, angry gestures, and racial epitaphs were coming from every part of the conference room. The captain raised his hand for silence and spoke.

"XO—after you finish with Lieutenant Johnson, could you have the captains of the escort ships conference with me?" Taylor said.

"Certainly, Captain," XO Lee said.

Bennett smirked. It was now the second time he had heard the XO sound like an XO.

"All right. There's nothing we can do about the *Manassas*. Hall? Why were they here?"

"Official reports were that they were transporting supplies, parts, and slaves to Fort Sumter, a garrison established just outside of Freeport Twelve, a very well-defended camp just inside of the mouth of the cavern complex in the Darvaza Major crater. Three things to note about Freeport. First, patricians are not welcome. You can pass through unharmed, but the population—ex-slave, plebs, surfers, long-standing colonists from other colonies—will not let patrician troops or any patrician visitors stay overnight. Secondly, the population is well armed with all kinds of weapons. They seemed well supplied from somewhere within the cave itself, and finally, Cassandra Kurtz's troops and those animals, the genetically altered canines and felines, have amnesty in Freeport."

"Are you shitting me? If Kurtz and these terrorists are in plain view, why don't we carpet-bomb them and be done with it?"

Captain Taylor shook his head no. He sighed and spoke in a low, deliberate voice.

"The warship *Saratoga* did just that four years ago. The town was obliterated. And then, another town just like it opened, except bigger and better placed from orbital strikes. We sent in land troops from three garrisons. Six hundred men went to clear it out. Eight men came out. That was Freeport Four. Every time we take one out, it costs us more than them. They sprout up more townships, in better defendable places, better armed and far more committed to winning than we are."

"The tactics and overall strategic war plan parallel ancient military documents and historical archives, a massive amount, citing Dien Bien Phu, Khe Sanh, and Afghanistan circa 1954 to 2012," Hall added.

"Specialist Hall, you gave the official report of why the *Manassas* was heading to Mars. Was there an unofficial reason?" Cooper asked.

"Yes, sir. The ship *Manassas* had an encrypted order for command officers. It noted taking on a specialist, Acting Captain Willard Bennett, to be released to find Cassandra

Kurtz while covertly being trailed by Special Forces to terminate all of Kurtz's command . . . and, well, including Acting Captain Bennett," Hall said. It was the first time she seemed uncomfortable.

The whole room was quiet. And while Bennett was shocked, he wasn't surprised.

"I'm guessing you were not aware of the entire plan," Taylor said.

"No, though I am not surprised. Still, my plan remains the same: Track her, find her, and kill her and the others," Bennett said.

There were nods of approval around the table with the exceptions of Captain Taylor and Specialist Hall. He was sure they didn't believe his bravado. He didn't either.

CHAPTER SIX

FOR A STORAGE ROOM converted into living quarters, Specialist Hall's accommodations were a mix of sleeping area, exercise room, ancient firearms, edge weapons, and something he had not seen for decades—books: old, well-worn, yellowed books, something no proper patrician would find in his home.

Well, this Betsy Hall is something different, he thought.

Bennett was baffled why Captain Taylor had him divert from the ship's armory and drop team to meet him in "XL-9: CMS Quartermaster Storage." He had passed this space several times on his walk and never really noticed it. His handprint and retinal scan allowed him entry, and if he had known it was someone's living space, he would have waited outside. Even though he had temporary social status and rank well over this Hall woman, his time in prison and limited privacy made him less inclined to encroach spaces not his own. It made him more protective of his own space too, more aware of how someone else might feel.

He thought about retreating and waiting outside when Hall arrived. She didn't seem surprised and started to chat as if they had been working colleagues for years.

"Ah, Captain Bennett. Captain Taylor told me you would be here. As requested, I have taken the liberty of outfitting both of us for our trek," she started. For someone brand-new to him, her familiarity was both presumptuous and unnerving.

Bennett put his hand up as a means of stopping the exchange from going any further, and she stopped immediately. Due to her prosthetic leg, she took another step to even out her stance as she halted too quickly.

"I'm sorry, Specialist Hall, but I don't know you, so could you tell me why the captain had me come here rather than to prepare with the others?" he asked.

If it weren't for the low reverberation of the ship engines, and the continuous electronic sounds everywhere, the room would have been silent.

"Well, do you trust Captain Taylor" she asked.

Bennett was confused by her response. In addition to her answering a question with a question, he was struck by the depth of the question, as simple as it was. He had to think.

Why do I trust the captain? As far as I know, he certainly has a moral code, honor, and duty. Clearly, he's a fighter if he must be. And those who don't like him seem linear and goal-oriented to their own egos, while those who do side with him seem competent and genuine. He's done things way differently than I would, but it works for him. It works well. I would still do things differently if I could. I mean, having no slaves on a ship to do the heavy work, and having more surfers and plebs in critical positions is outrageous, but his thinking is solid.

His thoughts were interrupted by Hall, who went on to explain why she'd asked the question.

"If you do, he probably wants you to be successful in your mission. And if you trust him, I hope you trust me."

Bennett nodded. She was logical.

"Who are you?" he asked.

She must have answered this particular question several times as her response was quick and succinct.

"I am Specialist Betsy Ann Hall from MAC–SOG, daughter of a patrician owner and plebeian housekeeper. My owner was kind to allow me freedom and education, but to remain in check. I could research and learn skills but never hold rank, vote, or marry upward. Freedom and limited access to privilege for silence," she explained.

More silence. A lot was explained in three sentences. Bennett felt as if he needed to ask another question, but her response was so personal, he had no idea what to ask until he looked down. A thought jumped to mind.

"What happened to your leg?"

"Hunting accident. OPCST—Off-Planet Colonial Survival Training. All done in Earth's atmosphere, out in the field. As I cannot officially enroll in military services, my owner allowed me to attend this five-year, off-grid survival-training camp. Many of us mixed breeds do this. Finding food and water for survival is a part of the immersive experience."

Bennett took a moment to absorb everything again. Every time he asked a question, ten others jumped to mind. He could have spent all shift asking her more questions but decided to simply trust her.

I guess that's why her question about my trusting the captain is so important, he thought.

As much as he wanted to, Bennett decided to ask the more important question as there was little time to prepare.

"Okay. Why am I here?"

Hall moved again, passed right by him to two nonmilitary-issued, semifull field packs sitting on her cot. She spoke as she filled each pack carefully.

"Not that I'm an expert in all things Freeport, but I'm betting that we would be better served if we used the same weapons, defensive and assaultive, as the residents. There have been reports of regular-issued energy weapons draining rapidly, either from natural causes or a defensive weapon. Since edge weapons are less of a thing with modern services, they will be handy if ammunition runs out, and we are up against other combatants or animals. Various adrenaline pills to stay awake and on the move in case things go sideways and rest is not an option. Compression undergarments in case it proves too hot and you don't want to go native. Plenty of protein bars and supplements, extra water bottles and purification pills, and shortwave radio in case comms go out and we are separated."

"And why are you doing this for me?" Bennett asked.

"Captain Taylor not only wants you to complete your mission but to keep you alive for human intelligence reasons. The other *Manassas* survivors in the cryo-tubes are patrician Special Forces—one group was to go with you while the other was to shadow you and kill you once the mission was done. Since they are going to join us, and the XO will be leading the troops, the captain wants at least one person he can trust to do their best to keep you alive," she said.

As she spoke, she packed all the things she had said, including double-edged daggers, updated gunpowder-propelled sidearms and rifles, and corresponding ammunition from 10mm for the sidearms and 7.62-caliber for the main weapon. While much older than new energy rifles, they were reliable. Based on the ammunition she'd stored in each pack, they would not be running out of bullets too soon.

"So, why do you do it? Why are you here and helping me?" Bennett asked. He wondered what was driving her to help. Blind loyalty to the captain? Did she want to escape to Freeport Twelve herself?

That's what I would do if I were her.

That question stopped her. She stood up a moment to think and, without looking at him, went back to her packing.

"Captain Taylor gave me a chance to serve. Gave me chances that no other patrician had ever given me. Loyalty, respect, and professionalism know no bounds, not class, race, or status. He treats me like he does the chief and doctor. He treats everyone that way. That is rare."

Bennett nodded. It was all true. It all made sense.

"And while the captain said I could ditch the mission and stay in Freeport, I agreed that I'd fulfill my assignment before I would ever consider that option," Hall added.

"What? Would that be, well, treason," Bennett said.

Before she could answer, part of the answer became clear to him.

"Well, it can't really be treason if you are a pleb with little to no rights," he said.

Fuck me. Logical and precise. Forget any hope of winning a debate with her, he thought.

"Yes, exactly. Also, he commissioned me upon success of my mission, which is your mission, to stay and study Freeport, possibly be a liaison in the future. Who knows?"

Hall finished packing and presented his pack. It was probably slightly over fifteen pounds, and it was to be worn as a butt pack. The weapons and gear were probably an additional ten pounds while the personal protection back and chest vest was far lighter than he had thought. He was impressed how she had packed the basics that could be used without the additional gear that was waiting for him in the armory. He took the protective gear and gave her a look.

"It is good for edge weapons including arrows and bullets, not for energy weapons. *If* we get by Freeport, there's a whole lot of danger between us and Kurtz."

"I thought they would let us go by unharmed," he said.

"If we don't provoke them, keep to ourselves, and focus on entering the cavern complex, we'll be fine. But based on my experience with the XO and others in his group, I know this is going to go sideways. You may need to be prepared to make peace if things go the way I fear," she said.

Hmm. She's right. She does have a lot of answers. Hard to dismiss.

Bennett nodded, feeling all his doubt and anxiety about working with Hall evaporating. Once again, he was putting his faith in Captain Taylor, a man he'd met roughly four weeks ago. Hall's presentation and logic also made sense.

"Okay, Specialist Hall, lead the way," Bennett said.

Hall seemed surprised. Just shy from taken aback. He was forgetting that she was not a full patrician like he was, or at least, before he was jailed.

"I only mean, lead the way to the flight deck," he said.

"Yes, sir," she said with some relief.

CHAPTER SEVEN

BENNETT WAS GETTING antsy just waiting for the flight deck to come alive. While twelve military packs were laid out in two rows, and Hall's and his own pack were waiting for them, separate from those for the soldiers, the occupants were not there.

"They are most likely doing a last-minute stand-up report to outline mission points. I would not be allowed. I think you would have been, but the XO runs his team's meeting, and it is unclear if he would let you join," Hall said.

"Figures. So, we just wait here waiting for them to show up. Great."

"Well, if you prefer to board the lander, your palm print and retinal scan should work for entry, and even to fly her, if you're qualified and updated," Hall offered.

"Huh? I thought I was authorized to nonessential access," Bennett asked.

"Normally, but if you are a patrician, and your rank is *acting* captain, then Captain Taylor probably reinstated your privileges on board. It looks like there were some things already authorized for you for the mission planet-side, but I'll bet the captain expanded it," she said.

As she spoke, Bennett had moved to the access ports and rested his eye against the scanner while laying his right palm on the digital reader. The door swished open without hesitation.

"It's a little scary that you've been right about nearly everything," Bennett said to Hall. A faint smile emerged on her face, and then she looked away.

"We should at least take our packs on board. I'd feel bad to have left them behind if they were packed for us. I'm curious what they have us taking down."

Bennett followed her lead, picked up his military pack, and moved onto the transport craft. Motion-detector lights turned on, and he found a seat right by the hatch. As he sat, he watched Hall casually walk to the back of the craft without hesitation. He felt at odds staying up front with the other patricians, who he was not sure were going to be helpful. They would accept him being in front because he was a patrician with temporary rank and status. At the same time, he had come to trust Hall. The discomfort of staying up front with empty chairs soon to be filled with "equals" was less compared to sitting in back with her and waiting for the others to arrive.

His inner mind flashed to his time at the Delta Exchange, the inequity and horror of it all.

He picked up his kit and material and moved to the adjoining seat next to Hall. After some rearranging, he was settled. Though he was slightly uncomfortable being back with her, the idea of just going along to get along, pretending everything was in its place in the natural order of things, was a worse feeling. This decision felt much better.

"You know," Hall said, "forward shielding from tip to midsection of nearly all shuttles and landing crafts is streamlined for aerodynamics, rather than shielding for protection. As a result, should we encounter a problem on landing, there is a much higher probability of survival back here where the shielding is more vigorous than up front."

Bennett looked at her. He was now simply curious about what went on in her head, though he did admire her ability to read the situation and how he was obviously conflicted.

"What do you think of the mission?" he asked. He was genuinely curious.

Without hesitation, whether it was because she was well practiced at explaining herself, or just aware of how she thought and it came easily to her, she answered.

"Off-Planet Colonial Survival Training in the toxic landscape of Earth's wilds for half my life does a good job prepping you to see danger well ahead of it, and you see worlds and people as dangerous places and things; keeping a mind to self-preservation and risk assessment becomes second nature," Hall said.

"So, if I stick with you, I'm more likely to stay alive?" Bennett asked. He was curious if she would be smug or matter-of-fact. As expected, Hall was not an easy read.

"Yes," she answered. No intonation connoting arrogance or subservience. No persuasiveness or pressure. Just an affirmation she was right.

"Glad I made the right choice," Bennett said.

If Hall was going to say anything more, the opportunity was lost. The drop troopers all entered the lander like high school football players entering the travel bus to the last off-campus game of the year. They were loud, obnoxious, and then they saw Bennett in the back with Hall. They were slightly curious, though not for long, and they were back in game-on mode.

XO Lee did a count of all team members in the craft and saw Bennett and Hall in the back. The XO did seem surprised that he and Hall were in the back together, or maybe that either one was there at all. When he was done with his count, and made some notation on his pad, he came back to talk to them, presumably to give an update if anything had changed.

"Good news—the atmosphere processors had a slight bump in efficiency, so air pressure and oxygen content has increased enough that lighter EVA suits are necessary. The bad news is that the atmosphere is thicker, leading to violent storms and choppy reentry."

"How's the drop zone?" Hall asked.

The XO glanced at her. He took his time and answered as if she had not asked the question at all but rather came up with his assessment in his report.

What a dick, Bennett thought. He wanted to say something to protect her, but he wondered why he felt he had to do so. He had never been supportive of plebs, surfers, and slaves.

What the hell is going on with me? Why do I care?

"Insertion will be a half mile to the town's gate. Scopes show that if we go in hot, we'll be slaughtered. For a township with plebs, surfs, and mixed-breeds, it's pretty well armed," Lee said.

Hall nodded, satisfied with the information and either ignoring the XO's insult or showing she didn't care.

Bennett couldn't help himself but gave a smirk at her response. The XO immediately looked at him and asked him a question.

"Why are *you* sitting with *her*?"

Bennett locked eyes with XO Lee. Why he trusted Hall over his own kind was implicit but unclear. Reasons ran through his head. He could tell the XO that the patrician judges and society had fucked him over and made him the scapegoat for the Kurtz situation. He could have said he had seen what his class has done to other human beings, the horrors and violence. He could say that he had been cast out and that he was to be disposed of like garbage as soon as the mission was done, so why sit with shits like them? He thought about citing how the XO was an asshole to people that were just trying to do their jobs. A brief thought came up about how he disliked his command style and that he could learn from Captain Taylor. There were so many reasons why he chose to sit with Hall and not his own kind. In the end, though, the answer was clear. He wanted to live.

"Statistically, I have a better chance of surviving back here if anything goes sideways with shielding on insertion," he said.

The XO looked back at him, clearly not expecting this answer. Whether it was because he believed this or the XO didn't have time to push him further, the XO moved up to the front of the landing shuttle.

The interior lights dimmed to low-level green lighting, the exterior blast shields covered the small portholes, and the engine powered up. The one drawback with being in the rear of the craft was that the engine's vibration seemed more intense than he expected. But then, this was the first time he had ever sat in the back.

"The reverberations will even out," Hall said.

How does she know what I'm thinking? Is it written on my face or something? Bennett thought.

"Hang on, everyone. We're dropping into glory and history!" XO Lee yelled out. The soldiers cheered him on.

Bennett's mind flashed to the screams of his own men years ago as he'd heard them fight and die, killed by genetic freaks that were once pets. And all because he wanted more. Cassandra was an easy mark, and they were all going to get rich. He'd wanted to kill her, but the drive to do that was gone. And time allowed him to think about his role. Nothing worse than self-reflection.

"We're dropping into hell," he said.

If Hall heard him, she didn't say anything. He kept his eyes forward and didn't look left or right. He had several thoughts about hoping the transport craft did have a catastrophic accident.

The shuttle's vertical ascent from the *Lee*'s flight deck and sudden velocity was swift, and the corresponding force was strong. He felt his body press into his seat. The vibrations increased and then did start to become less intense, just as Hall said they would.

"Here we go," Hall said.

PART 3

"Freedom. Freedom, Virgil. What you and I take for granted, all the other classes don't have."

CHAPTER EIGHT

BENNETT THOUGHT his experience with the transporter flight, the chop, pitch, roll and all, would be a walk in the park. After all, it wasn't his first mission drop, and the last time was on Mars, at the abandoned New Georgia site where he'd lost nearly his entire command team, and where Cassandra Kurtz had slipped away.

It was hard to forget that his men had been ripped to shreds by genetic experiments gone wrong and running amok. He could only hope that those missing from the crime scene, those who avoided the search long ago—some slaves, plebs, and his former ship's doctor—had met the same brutal end. Even thinking about it still made him angry. He had first heard the desperate orders, attacks from all sides, the energy fire in rapid succession, and then the screams. He could have just left, but those were his officers, Rommell, Richard, and the others, so he'd gone down himself to see what happened. Since then, he had often wished had hadn't. Severed heads with looks of terror etched on their faces. Fewer limbs than torsos, and more torsos than heads. Fresh blood patterns added to ones from weeks prior, nearly every wall covered with deep claws and laser scotches. But not one of those creatures was among the killing field. There was blood, a light pinkish streak, along with two fangs and one claw. Other than that, there was nothing left but to collect the human parts for burial in space and the creatures' parts for examination.

As disturbing as these thoughts were, they helped him deal with the severe chop. The XO's warning was accurate. It was very bumpy; there were times he was pressed deep by the restraints, and the buffeting was enough to make one of the soldiers throw up.

Poor guy. He's going to get shit for this by his pals, I bet, thought Bennett.

As Mars's atmosphere was thickening at an exponential rate, thanks to nanite atmosphere processors, reentry from space was going to be like reentering Earth's orbit someday. The mile walk to the settlement's gate was another matter. While Bennett had walked the *Robert E. Lee* for days getting exercise, it was different walking in an EVA suit, even a light one, on uneven land with shifting sands, rock, and buffeting winds. It made the trek slower. But his age and the lack of life-extending services were the greatest culprits that made him the slowest in the group, along with Specialist Hall. If it weren't for her prosthetic leg, and the XO's and others' disdain of her, she might be well ahead because of her experience, and athletic condition. The fact that she was on the mission was a testament to either her physical preparation or conviction, but more likely both.

The march itself might have been easier if it weren't for the headwind, stronger than any he'd felt on Earth, along with a sandblast that pelted him. The EVA suits had the advantage of being light, and in addition to carrying a thirty-pound military pack, the entire system would have worked well, but since he and Hall were packing additional poundage on their asses, it was difficult. If they'd had the heavier EVA suits, it would have been impossible to carry all of it.

The lighter suit did not protect him well against the brewing wind, sand, pebble, and stone that seemed to go right through him, and he was sure there would be a shit ton of bruising underneath it all. The inflated headgear made it easier on his shoulders, but again, whatever the wind carried, he felt it.

It was with some relief when he was standing in front of a massive gate to an even bigger wall assembled by nanite technology, the same mechanisms that consistently repaired and built up the massive atmosphere processors. He was hoping that if they were inside, they might find some relief from the wind.

The XO had done a decent job with the spacing, formation, and approach to Freeport's front entrance. With him, Hall, the XO, and five other guards, he kept the others in different groupings, undercover and in places Bennett could only assume were out of perfect line of sight for snipers.

"Should we knock?" Bennett asked.

"I'm not sure. That door is at least eighteen inches thick, and there are no apparent guards. While Bennett and the rest looked for some access point, electronic or otherwise, one of the soldiers pointed out a barely illuminated button.

The XO looked closely and gave the soldier a complement, or at least one that could have passed as a backhanded compliment. "Nice job, Johnson. You do a couple more of those discoveries, you might get your rank back."

"Yes, sir. Thank you, sir," he heard the man say.

The voice was unmistakable. It was hesitant and even less steady than the first time he had heard it when he'd frozen at the captain's orders earlier and another officer had to step in. In addition, the soldier's chest and stomach area, though sandblasted by the Martian winds, still held a brown vomit pattern from the flight down. Bennett looked over at Hall, and she gave him a knowing look. Former Lieutenant Virgil Johnson was in the insertion party, and he would more likely be cannon fodder if anything went wrong.

There was a loud buzz heard once XO Lee pushed the button. A green ring glowed around the button, and there was an immediate response.

"What do you want?" a strong female voice said. It was less of an ask and more of a demand.

The XO was visibly surprised. After all that had happened, Bennett was trying to accept that there was an entirely new order on Mars, so he kept telling himself, *Don't be surprised*. What was interesting was that Specialist Hall did not seem at all surprised.

"I am Executive Officer Robert Lee VI of the battleship *Robert E. Lee* and battle group demanding entry for inspection," the XO said.

More than thirty seconds went by. The XO was going to buzz again as there was no response and the ring was red, that is, until the voice came back, making the ring green. Same female voice, though it seemed lighter, almost pleasant.

"Seriously? You're demanding entry? No one asked you who the fuck you were, Pattie. I asked a fucking simple question. You're not here for an inspection. I'll give you five minutes to think about it. If you want entry, you better have a proper answer when I come back."

Bennett turned to Hall and mouthed the word *Pattie*.

"A slur," she said quietly.

Before the XO could say anything, the voice's laughter ended the exchange, and the green ring changed to back to red. The XO continued to press the intercom button, but there was no response. No voice. No green light.

Minutes clicked by, and five minutes had come and gone.

It was approaching fifteen minutes when Bennett took a chance to suggest a different approach.

"Hey, XO. I was thinking that it might be best to just tell this person that we want no problem, just passage to the cavern complex, and we'll be on our way. Maybe me, Hall, and a couple of guards would be all that's necessary. We could keep in contact with you on the service unless you wanted to lead the expedition, which I have no problem with," Bennett said.

"You are part of the objectives, but this is my mission. 'Gaining entry' is part of the process of obtaining intelligence, to find and return missing property, to eradicate this base and then go in and find that cunt," the XO said.

Bennett was surprised by the response. The level of animosity and hatred was palpable.

"Are you for real?" Bennett asked. He was genuinely shocked at not just the vitriol but the plan itself.

"They're not going to just let us walk in and take anything we want, even if they are escaped slaves. And they're not going to say, 'Okay, our fault; come on in' when we're out here and they are in there. All we need is safe passage to the cavern's entrance, and mission accomplished," Bennett said.

"If they don't, we'll rain down hellfire on them," XO said.

"Didn't the *Saratoga* try that? It didn't work then, and it's not going to work now. Is the Captain aware of this?" Bennett asked.

"He is aware that we asked for and attempted to gain entry, and if rebuffed, I am authorized to take it to the next level," the XO said.

"You didn't ask, you demanded! You jumped right to 'open the fuck up,' and you're wondering why we're still outside? This is bullshit! Captain Taylor is going to hear all about this, XO."

"No, he won't. We went dark ninety minutes ago, and all suit recordings will be redacted. And who is going to believe a has-been, washed-out, incompetent captain who couldn't control slaves, plebs, and a girl and allowed them to start a civil war?" the XO said.

Bennett closed the gap between himself and the XO. His fists were clenched, but he kept them to his sides, lest anyone think that he was going to kill him with his bare hands.

"Are you out of your fucking mind? These are not some backwoods, off-worlder colonists that arrived to make a better life for themselves! They stole and reconfigured a schooner, collided it with the *Manassas*, and sacked it. Look around, XO. We have less than the *Manassas* right now. We can't even get entry," Bennett said.

"XO, sir? I think you should . . ." Johnson started but was ignored as the XO carried on with his berating.

"This mission is whatever I say it is! And do you think they'll believe this disabled mixed-breed?" the XO said, jabbing his index finger at Hall as if his finger were a bayonet.

"XO, please, could you just listen to . . ." Hall started.

"Oh, what, *Specialist* Hall? What pearls of wisdom do you have?"

"Sir! Stop! Listen to me," Johnson said, more forcefully than he might have wanted.

The XO and Bennett were caught off guard. The XO was heated by his tirade, and Bennett was still debating on whether he should just shoot the XO with his antique weapon or break radio silence and inform Captain Taylor.

"Well? What, Johnson?" the XO said.

Johnson pointed behind the XO at the intercom light, which flashed green as opposed to the red light that had been on for their entire exchange.

"I don't know how long it's been on, sir," Johnson

explained. It was easy to see his eyes were wide, and his voice betrayed his fear.

"Ah, fuck me," Bennett said.

Suddenly, one of the well-placed groups, about two hundred feet away, well secured behind rocks and sand, came to life in all their headsets.

"XO—we show a fast bogie moving in on our position. It's metal, so it must be a transport. It's coming in on our left flank. We got it on scope, but we have no visual. Do you see anything?" the young man said.

The group by the gate grabbed their own scopes and binoculars to look where they were directed. Initially, there was nothing, but then it was clear that the sudden stirring of sand was moving toward them, not just Martian wind but something like a vehicle.

"I can't tell for sure, but it does look like a vehicle is stirring up dust and heading right toward you. Engage as hostile, and fire at will," the XO ordered.

Initially, Bennett was going to argue, but since it was more than probable that Freeport had heard everything that he and the XO said, the element of surprise was long dead, as was any extended future mission. Right now, because of his stupidity, and the XO, other soldiers were in danger.

"Stagger lines, and space them out. They're bunched up," Bennett said.

The XO did respond, but Bennett never heard what he said. His binoculars were tracking something he had never witnessed. Just in front of the speeding dust storm was a massive cat, maybe three times as large as a military ground-to-orbit fighter drone with missiles. This beast was outpacing the vehicle, sprinting to the point where it was hard to glean details. It was large, with six legs, and it looked like a massive tiger that once populated Earth. In mere seconds, it launched itself into the air before Bennett could comprehend what he was seeing.

He saw laser flashes shooting. At first, the lasers were directed level to the ground, and then up above them. Eventually, there was crossfire. The screams of orders broke quickly into chaos as each soldier transitioned from fighting as a unit to everyone for himself.

Bennett felt the pit of his stomach tighten like what he imagined a kinked hose would be under full pressure. The screams and voices sounded just like that last time years ago. At the same time, he couldn't look away. This monster was larger than pictures he had from years ago, and it was clearly fast. It pounced around several times, easily ducking and dodging the laser fire. It did so deftly, ripping off limbs like papier-mâché as the screams intensified and suddenly stopped. Even at a distance, the horror of watching other human beings die, soldiers trained for such violence, was still overwhelming. Bennett pulled the binoculars away, not wanting to see anything up close.

Two other large cats, just ahead of whatever was stirring up the dust, emerged and joined the bigger cat, brutalized some bodies along with the attacking creature, then fled parallel to the approaching vehicle.

"What the hell was that? Is that what attacked your men? Back in New Georgia?" Hall asked.

Bennett could only nod. It was just horrible. If he could have, he would have opened his suit's visor and thrown up. He looked at Johnson, who was fiddling with his headset. Bennett picked up his binoculars again and could now see that the dust trail had stopped where the carnage was located.

The dust storm stopped in front of where Bravo Team was stationed.

"Alpha Group—do you have a beat on Bravo Group?" the XO said.

"Yes, XO—hard to see through the dust. Thermals show four people. Looks like they are grabbing Bravo's supplies."

"Do you have a clean shot?" the XO said.

As much as he didn't like it, the XO's attempt in depriving the combatants of weapons and supplies was a long-standing procedure.

There was a few seconds' delay before he got an answer.

"Negative—they used the truck to obscure our direct line of sight. It's as if they knew exactly where we were and blocked a clear. They're leaving the area at a fast clip," the Alpha Team member said.

There was a long silence. Bennett felt drained. Memories of New Georgia, the rough ride down, and the forced march to a locked gate, culminating in tipping your hand to the enemy and watching young soldiers die for no reason.

"Shit," was all he could muster.

Hall dropped her binoculars before he did and had been looking in the opposite direction so as not to witness the horror firsthand.

Bennett was pulled out of his thoughts by the female voice he had heard earlier. It was menacing, cool, and distant, all at the same time. No anger, but clearly hatred.

"Okay, Patties, that is your only warning. Get the fuck out of here," the voice said. The green light turned red.

"Sir, I got Captain Taylor on comms. He's asking for a sitrep," Johnson said.

The XO, initially silent and still, erupted to life.

"He wants a sitrep? We were dark for this mission. How is he asking for a sitrep if comms were blacked out?" XO said. The fury and shock were equally distributed in his voice.

"I, um, I think I broke radio silence when I was trying to contact Bravo Team. I know Carson and just wanted . . ." Johnson said.

"Shut up, Johnson! Unbelievable! Shut off your comms, dumbass. I'll take it from here. Everyone—turn off your headgear," the XO.

Bennett shook his head; the irony was not lost on him. If it wasn't for Johnson breaking protocol, the insanity might have continued. An enraged and decisively beaten XO might have somehow made things worse. And with a seven-man fire group wiped out by some creature, and their supplies and weapons now in the enemy's hands, he figured that the XO's desire for revenge would be unsatiable.

As the XO turned around to report to the captain, Bennett felt a nudge from Hall. She handed him her mobile computer tablet that held a message:

> I have a direct line to Captain Taylor. We have no chance here. I read your reports about how Kurtz and all vanished from New Georgia. I'm guessing they escaped from there. The place has been abandoned since your last time there. I think we should go there and see if we can find the entrance she used to escape ourselves while the captain figures out what to do next. Do you think that's a good idea?

Bennett reread it, then read it again. After he fully comprehended what was going on—staying off comms and setting out on their own without the XO—he nodded. He handed her pad back so she could update the captain. Before she finished, he got her attention and pointed at Johnson, who was still looking at the carnage of Bravo Group, and then pointed to her and him. She mimicked the action, confirming that she understood that Johnson was to come with them.

CHAPTER NINE

THE MARTIAN DAY was in its twilight, making seeing, even with his enhanced visor imaging, difficult in the abandoned colony. New Georgia, once a thriving business port, was now a desolate, dark ghost town. For Bennett, he knew the place was haunted with the men he'd left behind. Adding to the haunting atmosphere was that their headlamps cut through the darkness and would throw off shadows. Rather than using their additional flashlights, they used one set until depletion before using their other set.

The place had been a wreck when he was there years ago, but now, much of the outer rim barriers were breached. He and his small task force, Hall and Johnson, had additional O_2 but not enough to last the night if they didn't find some part of the habitat that was still intact with breathable air.

Still, Bennett thought he was lucky that the XO did not literally drop them off, per Captain Taylor's orders, from a mile up instead. He might have done just that had the captain had not insisted on proof of life from the other team members.

Step after step in the empty colony had either some

debris from humans or sand and dust from Mars. Then he would see pieces of bones that stood out from the splintered wood, glass, metal, and plaster foam.

"Is this how you remember it, Captain Bennett?" Hall asked.

"I came in when there were lights, atmosphere was sealed in, and there was still equipment. There was also blood, limbs, and claw marks everywhere. I came down maybe ninety minutes after two insertion teams were attacked. That was a long time ago," Bennett said.

"It was those things that killed Carson, I mean, Bravo Team?" Johnson asked.

It was obvious the young officer never played poker, or if he did, he couldn't bluff to save his life.

"Yes," he said.

"Oh. Okay," Johnson said.

His voice still sounded afraid, but there was a tinge of resignation like, "Well, we're all going to die here" that concerned Bennett. Rather than letting Johnson's fear settle in and possibly take the entire team down, he decided to lead rather than respond. Hall calling him *Captain* also made him feel like a fraud, as he was not acting the part.

"All right, people, huddle up. Let's take a minute and review our situation," Bennett said suddenly.

It was obvious Hall and Johnson were taken by surprise, but they complied. With the glow of their pale green light for enhancing vision, Bennett organized his thinking and began what he hoped was a situation report with a plan.

"So, here we are—in an abandoned house of horrors that has been undisturbed for years based on the dust, dirt, lack of air, and not a single thing intact. We are easily fifteen miles from Freeport, and I am sure they are hunkered down waiting for a full-frontal assault rather than worrying about what might be happening here. Those creatures . . . that freakish cat was a lot bigger than what had been reported to me the first time, and there was no, well, freakish dog, so that is all new . . ."

"Including the breathing in open atmosphere?" Hall asked.

"Yes, that's new too. To sum up, we must get to the innermost ring, where the wealthy colonists kept their supplies, farthest from the exterior walls, and hopefully, there will be an intact space with atmosphere, so we don't die of asphyxiation. With me so far?"

Both Hall and Johnson said, "Yes."

"And about fear, well, it's normal to feel that way when things are not normal. If you weren't afraid, I wouldn't want you on this crazy expedition. We are looking for a place that has dangerous creatures waiting. If that happens, keep back-to-back, and let Hall and I use these antiques first and see if they do any damage before you light up the room with your laser rifle," Bennett told them both, but focused on Johnson.

"It was not weakness that made you reach out to Carson on Bravo Team. You were worried and did the human thing. Now I'm asking you to do the same thing with me and Hall. We're all on the same team. Rank means shit today, so call me *Bennett*, call her *Hall*, and I'll call you *V* for *Virgil*. So, are we all good right now? That's the plan?"

"Yes, sir," Johnson said, already forgetting to keep the names simple, without rank.

"So, if we accomplish finding breathable air, do we look for how Kurtz and her party disappeared from the base without a trace?" Hall asked.

"If we live that long, that's the next step. And if we find some passage to them, we track them, and find out where they went, and maybe where they are hiding. We are recon only. We won't engage unless pressed. Even if they have a five-year-plus head start on us through an alien landscape, filled with predators we have seen and not seen, we will take each step one at a time. We assess, evaluate, recon, and press on. Okay? Are we green? Find breathable air first?" Bennett asked.

"Absolutely. I'm good with that," Hall answered.

"Yes, sir," Johnson said again.

"Virgil, it's *Bennett*. *Willard*, if you want my first name," Bennett corrected.

"Yes. Ah, yes, Bennett," Virgil said.

"Okay. Press on," Bennett said.

Mere minutes after his speech, he wondered if Hall noticed he'd changed the parameters of his mission from "track her, find her, and kill her," to "track her, find her, and call for help." Even when he reviewed all the times he'd repeated his mission, he really had no heart in completing it. He was positive that he would die from something else other than a showdown with her, and even if they faced off, he knew he wouldn't survive. None of them would.

It was about seventy minutes later, when Bennett was sure they were all going to die then and there, that they came to a closed pressure door that he remembered from the last time he was there. He remembered collecting all the bodies and forensic material and then sealing the door with his biometrics. The door was still sealed, and that was a good thing; the area might still be well preserved with breathable air on the other side. The bad news was that the hand pad and eye scanner were without power.

Virgil gave a moan of anguish, already imagining how he was going to die slowly. Hall, on the other hand, produced a portable power supply in the form of a small brick battery and within less than a minute had power flowing to each instrument. The illuminated light and message requesting a handprint and eye scan were blood red, and then turned solid green. The large, sealed door cracked open but still required some force to pry open fully. The interior light came on once the door was halfway open, and they could see that the supply room appeared to be undisturbed. The light was short-lived, however. Whatever power there was left depleted, and the lights slowly dimmed, flickered, and went out.

The trio took their flashlights out in addition to their headlamps to do an immediate scan and make sure neither man or beast had severed the lights to kill or devour them. Once Bennett was sure that they were not in immediate danger of being ripped to shreds, he flashed the lights at Hall and Virgil, signaled them to wait a minute, then adjusted his light so he could keep it on himself while he took his helmet off to check the atmosphere. The light beam danced around the room for a few seconds as he pulled the helmet off and took some deep breaths, all the while pointing the light in his face so his two companions to see if he would live or die.

The first breaths were gulps and then he slowed down to smell. Unfortunately, the cryo-sleep had diminished that sense, so he really couldn't smell anything except staleness.

He nodded to the others with a thumbs-up, and they took their helmets off too. Unlike him, they took their helmets off with ease and breathed in the air without panicking.

"What do you smell?" Bennett asked.

"Kind of stale air," Hall said.

"Yeah, I was going to say, 'Old air,' like a closet in summer," Virgil said.

With the headgear off, the beams of light turned in three different directions to scan the room in unison. From what Bennett remembered, the place looked just as it did before. The supply room had been nearly empty, but the chairs, tipped-over tables and desk, and old cabinets were all still there and intact. After some time, Benntt could tell that the air was dry, but there was nothing foul about it.

"Well, part one accomplished. Breathable air. Next, recon the place, take inventory, and stay alive. Sound good?" Bennett asked.

"Works for me," Hall said. She was nearly out of her EVA suit and was dropping gear and pulling out her motion detectors and mounting them on the rifles. Her sidearm and serrated combat knife were already attached under her suit, and she moved in one direction to survey the area.

"Yes," Virgil said. He too was getting out of his EVA suit more slowly.

Bennett was ahead of him, affixing his tactical gear from his butt pack to his waist. He checked on rounds, took the rifle that Hall left for him, and then went the opposite direction to Hall to search. He hoped Virgil would do something similar.

Other than the footsteps of the others, the place was silent. Bennett focused on the mission at hand but still had multiple flashes of the last time he was in this room, which, compared to the adjacent room where his teams were slaughtered, was profoundly better by comparison. He pushed the images out of his head and focused on establishing a search grid pattern in his head to keep count of the areas he'd already looked and decide what was next. Without overhead lights, it was easy to lose his bearings. He looked back at times to see where the others were, easily spotting their flashlights cutting through the pitch-black space.

It might have been an hour since their arrival in the room when Bennett found what looked like a makeshift bed of hardened cardboard. The edges of the cardboard were turned up due to the dry air, which was why he first noticed it. When Bennett investigated the bedding, he discovered that it was not a lair at all but simply a makeshift covering.

As he pulled more of the material coverings off, he saw the tunnel entrance, right against the back wall. With all the debris on the floor, and the covers in place by the far wall, it was well camouflaged if you were quickly looking for something or if you were scanning the area from the middle of the room.

"Shit," Bennett said. He had said it louder than he thought.

"You okay?" Hall asked.

"Yup. Just annoyed. I found how they escaped this room. I found their tunnel," Bennett said.

He heard Hall and Virgil approaching with their light beams dancing from behind. Finally, with all three pointing their lights toward the hole in the floor, it was easy to see how Kurtz and her crew escaped, seemingly without a trace.

"Wow. They really did find a way out of this room," Hall said.

"Yup. And if I had spent more time searching this room when I was here last, I would have found it too, and maybe put an end to this shit before it even started," Bennett added.

It was a bitter pill to swallow. He was so focused on retrieving the dead, assuming that Kurtz and the doctor were among the body parts, and in such a hurry to leave, that he'd overlooked their obvious escape route.

"A fucking hole by the far wall. I can't believe I missed this," Bennett said.

Their lights focused on the hole. Bennett took some of his own advice and pushed the memories out of his head to concentrate on what to do next.

"All right," he said. "We need to get some sleep before we head down. Three-hour shifts on watch. I'll take the first, Hall second, and Virgil third."

"No, sir. I'm the junior officer. I'll take the guard, and you two rest," Virgil said.

Hall and Bennett gave him a curious look, which he obviously interpreted correctly.

"I'm the junior officer. I should have been the one to take my helmet off first to check the air, and I should be the one to take first watch—all night, for that matter," Virgil explained.

Bennett burst into laughter, which surprised his companions.

"Virgil, I was totally out of air, so that's why I took my helmet off first. And since I did away with rank for now, there is no designated shift in place. Also, since I missed this years ago, I'd like to sit in silence and ponder how my fuckup has blown out of control. I would like to brood about it now, alone, so I might be able to sleep later. You understand," Bennett said.

Bennett could see that Virgil fully grasped the idea of failing and then stewing. He heard Hall chuckle, and she was already taking pieces of cardboard to sleep. Whether it was Bennett's parable or Hall's lack of interest, Virgil read the room.

"Yes, sir," he said.

"Good," Bennett said.

Bennett took his own piece of cardboard, then moved to the back of the wall, allowing a view of the hole's entrance and the breadth of the entire room. Once he heard Virgil settle in, and some snoring from Hall, he did a quick sweep of the room. He looked at his chronometer and scheduled how many times he would use his light to scan the area so he would know when it would be three hours, which added up to about twelve times to scan. Once done, he turned off his light, and the room fell black.

He had hoped that he would not perseverate on the past, but he did. It was a long three hours of reviewing every time he had missed something and fucked up. Getting up to do a quick perimeter search ended up being a great distraction from sitting awake, brooding in the dark.

Not tired, Bennett did fourteen- to fifteen-minute sweeps rather than twelve before waking up Hall. After a quick sitrep, he laid down on his "bed" and figured he was going to stay up for another shift, calculating how many times he could have made different decisions. Fortunately, that was not the case. Sleep quickly crept in and swallowed him up.

CHAPTER TEN

"ARE you doing all right there, Virgil?" Bennett asked.

There was a bit of coughing, and then he heard him try to spit in a prone position in a cramped tunnel.

"I'm good, sir," Virgil said.

"Good," Bennett said more to himself than to anyone else. The descent into the tunnels was a command decision by Captain Taylor and himself. With potentially one last chance to communicate with the *Lee* before Martian rock blocked the signal, Taylor agreed that he would send a team down to follow once they'd dealt with the debacle at Freeport. To say that Taylor was annoyed with his XO would be an understatement, and the captain wanted to make peace with the town to gain entry through the town's front door. If Kurtz was there, he could secure the front end, and while they were stalled outside the gate, she would hopefully think she was not being pursued from her previous escape route years ago. Since Bennett and his team seemingly had flown by New Georgia, Kurtz would not think that they'd spent the night for this early morning mission.

Who in their right mind would do something like that? he thought.

Bennett was wondering if it had been a promising idea to take this route at all. While the descent was not steep, the confined space was uneven. It did not allow for easy crawling on hands and knees; rather, there was sliding, stopping, changing positions to crawl when possible, and then back again for more sliding on their stomachs, face-first. It was difficult for him, and he had no idea how he would have done it if he'd had the heavier pack. He had no idea how Lieutenant Thomas made it, if he'd gotten that far, or how the much bigger pleb Gavin, who was confirmed to be alive, managed this rathole. There were times when he had to stop to allow Hall to shift her balance, as her prosthetic leg was not as flexible as natural knees. And then there was Virgil, who was younger, nowhere near as big as Gavin and not as small as Hall, who was struggling more than either of them.

After some time, there was a discussion about what fork in the tunnel to take. One tunnel was larger, ostensibly easier to maneuver based on the opening, while the other looked as tight as the ones they were in, or maybe even tighter. Bennett found himself wanting to take the larger one for the wrong reason: the thought that passage would be much smoother. Virgil was all-in on that idea. Hall said she wanted to go the larger route too, but she mused that the least appealing approach was probably the best one. "It would be my luck that the bigger one is for those genetically engineered canines and felines," she said.

Ultimately, Bennett went with Hall's thinking; he knew the smaller tunnel would be a pain in the ass, but at least they wouldn't be cornered by one of those genetic freaks. He heard Virgil sigh, say, "Yes, sir," and take up the rear. The descent continued. It was slow going with the gear, and the fanny packs that Hall had put together came in great use, while the oversize packs from the *Lee*'s armory and quarter chief had to be left behind except for a mere few things take with them. Bennett could smell dust and dirt and felt the compactness of flat stones, or maybe it was Martian clay that was not as jagged as he had originally thought. There were times there was more width than expected, and other times it was just too tight a squeeze.

Bennett had also lost track of time. He thought they were up to their eleventh rest break when he started feeling little breezes, warm and not refreshing, coming up through the tunnel. The rest stops to sip water and stay still were, well, wonderful until it was time to move again. And the pace they took was so slow, Bennett wondered if they were simply in hell, forever trapped to move thorough this tunnel with brief respites but damned to continue with the arduous task. Bennett tried to keep those thoughts out of his head as he felt there could be a lot he could be damned for. While thinking about it now made sense, and at least it kept him from panicking about a tunnel collapse, he had to confess he had been feeling bad for some of the things he had done long before the *Robert E. Lee* found him on the decimated *Manassas*. It was extremely hard for him to admit to he would have done a lot of things differently.

Time in prison does change a man. Seeing what Cassandra saw as a child can fuck you up too. So can age, he had thought when he was feeling shame and guilt.

Also, he was sure that if he had his patrician status and life-extending benefits, there might be a chance this guilt might fall away. But at these moments, when he could smell dust and dirt and felt the compactness of flat stones, or Martian clay, he wondered if he had already irrevocably changed. Captain Taylor was a different captain from him, a good captain. His doctor and chief engineer seemed to be in a close alliance with him, friends even, which was different from his relationship with his command team, Richards and Rommel. He thought they were friends, but seeing Captain Taylor and his guys had him rethinking their closeness. To top it off, while he could understand XO Lee's motivations and tactics, he disliked him more than he thought he would. Bennett knew the things he had said and what he had done were no different from the XO, but he nonetheless he hoped never to see him again. It was an ugly reflection.

Shit. Is it the heat or darkness or both? Even the air feels heavy, he thought.

More thoughts filtered in as he traveled in the dark. With just glow sticks illuminating the way, the pitch-black allowed, almost encouraged, more existential thoughts. They flooded him. If it weren't for Hall's slight uptick in mood and extra space on his sides and head, he would not have been able to keep the negativity at bay. In addition to the tight space, dust, dirt, and aches, the lack of light to see where he was going was unnerving. To conserve energy, they agreed that Hall would periodically use her headlamp to see what was ahead, and it was only her glow stick that would signal the others where she was going. After a while, Bennett took his headlamp off so that he would not be tempted to use it. His bald head was pouring sweat and dripped into his eyes.

That's it! Once I'm out of this shit tunnel, I'm shaving this shit off, he promised himself.

More space opened farther ahead, and there was more heat as well. Throughout the journey, he had been wondering when the oxygen was going to run out. Hall and Virgil were hesitant to leave the EVA gear behind, but Cassandra and her group didn't have any when they took this route. He figured if they left theirs behind too, they would *probably* make it. Years ago, he would not have chanced it. But now, he was trying to trust his eyes, experiences, and hunches more.

More time passed, fewer rest stops, more space and heat, and incremental decreases in darkness made him feel a little hopeful. Finally, he heard Hall yell out to him and Virgil some good news: "It's hot as shit down here, but I can stand. There's an opening farther down, but we might be coming to an end."

"Finally," he heard Virgil say.

"Agreed. How Kurtz and her people made it down here is beyond me," Bennett said.

He put his headlamp back on in anticipation that he might be standing soon.

It took longer than he had expected to reach Hall. She must have been much farther along than he had realized. By the time he was able to stand outside the tunnel into a large cave, his first sight was her adjusting and cleaning her prosthetic leg.

"You okay?" Bennett asked.

Hall talked without looking at him while continuing to meticulously treat small scratches and openings on her knees, with an emphasis on the amputated leg where the artificial limb was attached. His lamp cut through the darkness like a solid beam of light as if it were a physical sword cutting through dark wood. The light photons reached a clearly visible limit, a tight beam, as if the blackness was a physical object walling the light beams in a tight boundary. Bennett saw that it was not just his headlamp but the others as well. He was trying to understand the light and darkness of the place when he heard Hall answering his question.

"Yup, doing all right. Same thing happened to me when I was at the former North American Carlsbad Caverns, and a sinkhole dropped me and my squad. The fall was bad enough, but the crawling really did a number of my knees.

Since then, I know scratches like these need to be taken care of as soon as possible. You better check yourself and Vigil," she said.

Bennett heeded her advice, as did Virgil. One advantage with the darkness was the light brightly illuminated everything it focused on.

"So, how did you get that kind of training?" Virgil asked. It was an obvious question since she was not a patrician, and patrician women focused on procreation, not dangerous adventures.

"Long story, but I was trained for OPCST—Off-Planet Colonial Survival Training. Today, it proved to be especially useful," she said as she continued medical treatment.

There was a bit of silence while he inspected himself and did all kinds of stretching to see if some aches and stiffness might find relief. Suddenly, he opened his pack, did a quick search, and found a small vial of concentrated shaving cream. He applied it to his head and let it expand. Once ready, he shaved his head.

"Much better," he said when he was done.

Just as suddenly as the thought to shave his head, Bennett had another thought. The old Bennett might have assumed Hall would have truly little to add, like the XO did because of her gender and class. But from the very beginning, Hall had been nothing but dead-on with her suggestions, providing details vital to his own survival. He was coming to believe there really wasn't a dumb question. It was dumb not to ask it.

"What happened to your squad? Did you all make it?" Bennett asked.

This time, Hall did look up, her light briefly blinding him until she looked away. For the first time, she seemed surprised. Like him and Virgil, she was dusty, dirty, and clearly fatigued, but the look in her eyes was unmistakable. There was a glint of curiosity.

She leaned back on her good leg before she spoke.

"Huh. Why do you ask?" she said.

Bennett wished he could have thought of a clinical reason or a tactical point to his knowing, but he really didn't have one, so he went with the truth.

"I think I'm just curious," he said.

For the first time ever, he thought he saw her smile; rather, it was a smirk, he corrected.

He was looking at her in such a way as not to blind her with direct light, but it was difficult as the beams of light allowed almost no spillage.

She gave it a moment before she answered.

"Eight of us went in the hole; five came out. I got sepsis and almost died. I was found two, maybe three days later, and was mistaken for a full-blood patrician, so I got immediate treatment."

"Oh. Did the rest of your team get treatment too?" Virgil asked.

"Nope. They left me behind with the other three that died in the fall or shortly after. I was slowing them down, and it was easy to see I wasn't going to make it," she said.

"Who found you?" Bennett asked. He had an idea, but of late, he had been asking more questions, even if he thought he already knew the answer.

Another effect of prison, he thought.

"It was a patrician lieutenant on leave with a group of his friends. They made the mistake and not only fixed me up but treated a few things I didn't know was wrong."

As she spoke, Hall was back to multitasking—she pulled her rifle out to check the light with the attached motion detector, then went into her pack to retrieve a folding stock. She pulled out her antique handgun, fitted the stock, and now the sidearm was a short-barrel carbine. After she did it, she got up and handed it to Virgil.

"I have no idea if your issued laser rifle will work in the long run, but I know this will," she said.

It all became clear to Bennett why Captain Taylor had such admiration for Hall. Based on the captain's character and his sense of people, Bennett could see why he would like someone like her.

"Wow. Did you ever find out who those guys were?" Virgil asked.

A chortle, just short of a laugh and far more than a giggle, emerged from Hall.

"It's a good thing you have good looks, Virgil," she said.

She didn't wait for a response, leaving Virgil looking back and forth between Hall and Bennett with the "what did I say?" look.

"Okay, Virgil. A couple of things. First, Captain Taylor and I'm guessing the doctor and Chief Engineer Cooper were the ones that found her. Secondly, shoulder your laser rifle for now, and let me show you how this gunpower antique works: range, strengths and barriers. Are you ready?" Bennett asked.

To his credit, Virgil sighed, nodded that he was slower than usual, and complied.

"Yes, sir. Thank you, sir," he said.

"No problem, Virgil. We all are new at some point. Live long enough, and it all becomes clearer," Bennett said.

While Virgil was slow on figuring out social cues and obvious body language, it took him seconds to transition from a high-tech laser rifle, the state-of-the-art main firearm of an advance military machine, to one that used gunpowder, physical shells, and gas propellent. Bennett was pleased.

Once Virgil was done, he heard Hall call out to him.

"Wow! Come and see this," she said.

Her light was barely visible. He wondered how she'd gotten so far away, but he realized that her headlamp might have been directed away, since she sounded close. Bennett nodded to himself and slapped Virgil on the shoulder for encouragement.

"Let's go see what Hall is excited about. Hopefully, it's something better than caves and tunnels."

"I hope so, sir," Virgil said.

CHAPTER ELEVEN

"WHAT THE HELL IS THIS?" Bennett said.

Blood-red, molten rivers branched out in multiple directions from the distant volcanoes. The only light that seemed available was from these flows, embers, and heat vents. Far from pitch black, the environment was dark, very dark, and it threw off midnight blue shadows from the massive plant life below, the boulders, and distant lakes. These lakes might have been oceans, as Bennett had trouble gauging the scale of this dark, enclosed environment. And it was hard to say if those lakes or oceans were bodies of water, if they were frozen nitrogen, or if they were something that looked like water from this distance. The sight was that of a hellscape. For the first time, Bennett was happy his sense of smell was diminished as he was sure that the pungent aroma of sulfuric acid and the putrid stench of dead and dying plants and animals were all around them. Virgil covered his nose to confirm his suspicion.

Bennett took his time surveying the entire area from their vista. If there was a ceiling, he couldn't see it except for the massive stalactites hanging like sword blades above them. The molten rivers and a carpet of shadows that might have been vegetation were about two hundred feet below him. Fortunately, it was not a sheer drop, but it did look steep. Like the tunnels and the cave, the boundaries between light and darkness were clearly marked—as in darker and less dark—making the images visible due to the contrast of the black background.

The only other competing experiences were the persistent heat, dry and hot, and the vibrating ground, as if there were a perpetually running a heavy tractor or other earth-moving machine right beside them. How it felt like an extended aftershock of a Mars quake was beyond his understanding.

"I thought I've seen everything," Hall said. Her stoic, clinical presentation seemed to have dropped, and the more expressive wonder of a child was present.

Bennett turned to Virgil, who had a similar look of curiosity. The alien world, with competing stimuli and assault to the senses, was overwhelming.

"How the hell can there be air here?" Bennett said.

"My wild-ass explanation is that it's from trapped permafrost, limestone, volcanic heat, and a lot more chemical interactions in a closed system that we don't have a clue about. There are reports that nanites also played a significant role too," Hall answered.

There was a moment of silence before Bennett spoke again.

"Well, your explanation sounds good," he said.

"I struggle with saying, 'I don't know' whenever I have a theory, no matter how crazy it sounds," Hall said.

"Keep doing that. This place is a crazy place, so I'd rather have a crazy-ass theory or idea than a 'I don't have a clue,'" he said.

Bennett shook his head as a way of breaking the trance and began the process of looking through his pack for some water and his ration bar. This was the first time he was able to take a bite of his protein square in hours, and he was positive he was going to need that and a sip of water to make the climb down. He watched Hall also break her scanning of the environment to search her pack, though he was at a loss of what she was looking for. Virgil was just staring at it all.

For better or for worse, the acidic atmosphere's smell was making headway in his nostrils, though he was sure it was less than his peers. He felt bad for them, though he imagined it could have been much worse, like no air at all.

He did his best to see if there were any skylights to the surface, but there were none.

"Back on the *Davis*, their engineer told me and my doctor that the nanites that were building the atmosphere processors were operating at an efficiency deficit outside expected parameters. He wondered if some of those nanites at the surface were going underground, creating a similar atmospheric process below the surface in caverns like this," Bennett said.

"That confirms what I had read from the after-action reports and sentries out here looking for Kurtz. Two groups found two plants, all upside down, hanging from the ceiling occupying the same footprint as the facility above them, as if it were a mirror. It sounded crazy then, but after seeing this . . ." Hall said with a wave of her hand, "it all seems true."

This is crazy! This sight alone is worth the price of admission, he thought.

Bennett continued chewing his bar and took a sip of very warm water. It had no effect on slowing his thinking as he processed what she'd said.

"You have access to operations looking for Kurtz," Bennett asked.

"Yes," she said without hesitation. He wondered if Hall was going to remain cryptic, but she had to understand why Bennett would be curious, if not worried, that she had more intel than he would.

"Once it was clear that the *Manassas* was attacked and that these rebels were more dangerous than expected based on their escalations, the admiralty promoted Captain Taylor to Fleet Captain and reassigned him to the *Robert E. Lee* to run a task force to search, recon, find, and destroy Kurtz and her command structure. As a result, he gave me the task of knowing everything there was to know about Mars, Kurtz, and the whole operation," she said.

"I never saw you on the *Lee*," Virgil said, now listening to their conversation.

"I was behind locked doors, out of sight so I could focus on my job. I would meet with Captain Taylor, the chief, the doctor, and the head of security, Grisson," she said.

"So, in addition to taking over the *Robert E. Lee* and running the task force, Captain Taylor stowed you on board without the XO and key command section leaders' knowledge, and you were running an operation right under his nose. No wonder the XO is perpetually pissed off at anything the captain does," Bennett said.

"Any one of those things alone could have done that, but all three had to be insult to injury," Hall said, displaying a high degree of empathy for a guy who was an extreme asshole to her and the captain, ostensibly her friend.

Hair gone, stomach feeling sated, the warm water hitting the spot, and the heat being a dry heat, Bennett felt much better, compared to being in the tunnels. He wiped the fresh beads of sweat where his hair used to be and let the small towel lie on his shoulders. He reshuffled his pack, then readjusted his kit, ammo, and belt rig, checking to make sure all firearms were loaded with one in the hole and the safety off.

"So, I'm guessing there's a reason for why you prefer these firearms over the laser ones," Bennett asked.

"Prior recon and stationed outposts here indicate that the laser rifles lose power and break down more frequently in this environment than these weapons. Minimal maintenance was required here," she said.

Hall was also pushing her larger tank of O_2 and her entire EVA suit aside and took the self-contained water pouch and the urine container out, all ostensibly for water usage.

"Oxygen won't be an issue, but dehydration will be. I would have packed more water and containers if I knew we would be on our own. I recommend you drink sparingly, and we'll have to get to those lakes to see if they are water basins, and if it is drinkable," Hall added.

Virgil looked at Bennett to see if he should be complying with Hall's suggestions, which were easy to interpret as orders. Bennett nodded.

"Anything she says, I would take at face value. She's been right about everything, and there's no rank down here. We are on our own, and we need each other. If you see something off or important, shout it out. We good, Virgil?" Bennett asked.

"Yes, sir," he said.

Bennett went back to rearranging his kit, readjusted his headlamp with the plan of minimal use, if possible, in the hopes that the environs were less dark than the tunnels they'd traversed. Without the EVA suit, O_2 tank, filters, and such, there was far less to carry. And now, he was looking for a way off the plateau, though he was not at all sure where they were all going. As if reading his mind, Hall shared her plan. She pulled Virgil over to where Bennett was and pointed to two glowing mountaintops, unusually close together than the rest, and gave her report for next steps.

"Transmission from our forward recon post last week indicated Kurtz and her team were all over the place, from just outside the wire to beyond Echo outpost at the foothills of that mountain range between those two volcanos. Alpha outpost, Fort Deadly, thinks Kurtz and crew were heading there to set up a defense base, or they were just looking to give them the slip. It's all unclear, and the data is a week-old human intel. But unless you have any strong opinions, I would suggest linking up with our recon, if possible, and heading to that location."

"There's actually ground forces here?" Virgil asked.

"Yes. Typically, the Plebian Auxiliary Corps would have been the first choice, but the last three insertion teams that were in the field went native and joined her side," Hall said. Her matter-of-fact, emotionless report was unsettling.

"What? The plebs turned?" Virgil asked.

"Yes. I think, well, I can imagine that Kurtz offered them something that was more appealing in this hellhole than they had back on Earth and above the surface, I guess," Hall said. Whether it was the heat, the fatigue, or the anxiety of the journey ahead, Hall was less definitive and seemingly using her gut.

"Are you kidding? What could she offer them here that they couldn't get from service in the armed forces and colonies above?" Virgil asked.

For Bennett, the answer was obvious.

"Freedom. Freedom, Virgil. What you and I take for granted, all the other classes don't have."

Hall looked at him. It was a look that was curious. She must have wondered how a patrician like him would know the ultimate plight of anyone less. She clearly considered Taylor and his immediate team as being capable of empathy, but she must have seen them as one-offs. Now there was him. Bennett wished he was like Taylor, the doctor, and the chief engineer, but his learning came from the experience of being deprived of freedom himself, and not through some altruistic premise he was sure Taylor and his crew possessed.

"Being in prison has a way of teaching you some things. Not looking and not seeing the underbelly of a caste system makes it easy to believe all is fine, and everyone—slaves and all nonpatricians—are happy. If it weren't for that, I might have been just as clueless," Bennett explained.

"And from a practical point of view, I can easily see why it would be better to be free in hell than a servant above," he added. That second thought was something he remembered reading a long time ago, maybe as a child, but he couldn't recall it now.

"Okay," was all Hall said.

After a moment of uncomfortable silence, Bennett looked around for a way down from the plateau to the jungle. It was Virgil who found it first. His younger eyes would be an advantage to them in addition to Hall's intel on everything Kurtz.

When Bennett was in prison, he'd fantasized about his sentence being commuted and having his rank reinstated with the focus of finding and killing Cassandra Kurtz. He imagined a triumphant return to Mars with three platoons of special-ops search-and-destroy specialists, fully recovered from medical treatments, hair and all, setting foot on the descent into hell to find that rogue element of chaos, and to bring her years of terror and disruption to a crashing end.

Fuck Delta Exchange, he thought.

Prison, shame, and seeing that place really made it difficult to hate Kurtz.

"Virgil—you got point. Watch your step, and be careful. We need your eyes. Hall, you're in the middle, and I'm in the rear," he heard himself say.

"Shouldn't I be on point?" Hall asked.

"You and your intel are too important to lose. Nothing personal, Virgil, but if you or I die, Hall will make it out. If she dies, we're done," he explained.

"Yes, sir. Agreed, sir," Virgil said.

So. Here we go, Bennett thought.

PART 4

". . . I've seen the horror you've seen. I've seen what powerful people do to others without consequences. Without limitation, checks, and balances . . ."

CHAPTER TWELVE

Bennett, Willard
  Acting Captain
  MAC–SOG
  ETZ: 13:40
  Day 2 since tunnel exit
  Hall, B. A.— Specialist
  Johnson, Virgil—LT, Robert E. Lee

Begin entry:
  This place continues to be a hot, dry, strange underworld. I had heard that the rogue nanites had unintentionally reproduced air processing stations, but I never thought I would see a fully built structure erected on its side underground. It's as if one of the surface structures were picked up and then carefully placed on its side, and still somehow functions perfectly. And while there are outlines for entrances, exits, and windows, there are no working ways to get in. If there was time, I would spend all day seeing how

the nanites arranged the inside, if we could. And if these miniature workhorses have accidentally built these, where does it end? That strange sight was three hours ago. Virgil had to borrow my binoculars because he broke his; he thinks he saw a smaller nanite air processor on the low-hanging ceiling off a cliff face, upside down. It's crazy here.

Sleeping slightly improved once we ditched and stowed most of our outer garments and used them more for bedding than wearing. It never gets cold here, and the closer you are to the lava rivers, the fewer insects and predators there are, but it is stifling hot. So, we sleep by the lava and travel deeper into the mushroom forest, where it is darker but cooler.

These "forests" are the strangest I have ever seen, or rather, read or seen online. It's as if we've shrunk and are in a mushroom patch on Earth. The insects that are five to twelve inches long don't seem to care about us but rather feast on these massive mushrooms. The two times they looked as if they were going to turn on us were when they smelled blood and when we got in their way. Hall said they reminded her of old images of sea creatures called lobsters and crabs and are similar in size. Hall also showed me reports of forward-operating teams capturing and eating these things with no ill effect. We'll continue to use our rations for a while.

Water pools, offshoots from the lakes that are closest to the heat vents and lava pits, are hot as hell but devoid of bacteria, viruses, or parasites. We have water: boiling hot water.

We have heard and witnessed massive feline and canine creatures here. They all have six limbs, and their tails have evolved to a near-prehensile ability in picking up things. They are larger than we thought. They also seem to be blind, in that they navigate well in this dark, hot world, but they hate the heat, don't seem to like the little light the lava throws off, and they have a hard time finding those insects when *they are closest to the warm riverbank and covered with silt or mud. Hall agrees that these creatures might "see" infrared. So, keeping by the lava or being covered in mud to reduce our body temperature might cloak us. This confirms Alpha and Gamma's reports of run-ins with these things at night.*

While these genetic monsters are an ever-present danger in addition to any bacteria, viruses, or parasites, it is the perpetual darkness that is most difficult to adjust to. The heat took time to get used to, but the darkness . . . There's never enough light to see more than shadows, just enough to "see" danger everywhere. Never-ending, filling the horizon, and broken up by hot red-yellow lava and some luminescent stalactites, the darkness has weight. A heavy weight. I now understand what Kurtz meant in one of her transmissions about the "heavy weight of darkness killed them." It sounded crazy then, but now I can see how and why.

We saw Alpha Post from an elevated position. It was surprising to find it far away from the lava river, but it seemed highly active with patrols and other movements. The plan of approach will be me, Virgil, and then Hall. I can only assume that these guys have been underground with limited outside contact, so they may not even know we're coming. Hopefully, full contact will go well.

End entry.

BENNETT TOOK a moment to review his log and correct the written document on the computer pad Hall had been toting around. He had not thought about bringing his own device for mission record, so he took Hall's tablet from the beginning of the trek to document the mission. And while transmitting to the *Lee* was not remotely possible due to layers of rock and some additional atmospheric interference, his transmission was uploaded to all their dog tags that were outfitted for wireless storage. So, even if the tablet was destroyed, all data that was recorded and uploaded would be retrievable from the military and civilian tags around each of their necks.

For a moment, he could see his reflection from the pad's dark screen, or the shadow of a reflection on his face. He worked at different angles to look, and he thought that he looked just a bit younger, more athletic. While his shaved head showed some hair growth, like his chin, there would be no risk of long hair in this place. Virgil took his lead and had also shaved his head. Hall, who kept her hair short from the beginning, made no changes.

Bennett handed Hall her tablet once he was done. She took a moment to make notes on some of the other things she had observed—varying degrees of dirt and sand texture, the smell of water under the massive mushroom patches, and examples of when the insects kept clear of the lava rivers. There were also some flying, three-foot creatures she and Virgil saw right before entering or exiting the mushroom canopy.

Fact is stranger than fiction in the hellhole. Nothing I could drink or take could have me imagine a place like this, Bennett thought.

Bennett was hopeful that all the outposts were solidly established, stocked, and prepped to maintain lines of communication and supplies. He was also hopeful that the wireless connection from Hall's computer pad might be picked up the closer they got to Alpha outpost. Hopefully, the soldiers might receive the reports, and send out a welcome committee or meet them halfway. In a place like this, Bennett didn't want to surprise a group of patrician men. If they had their dog tags set for receiving data, it would be great news. The data Hall and they were collecting was far more scientific in nature, and this might have been how Hall was able to gain so much intel for their present mission.

Taylor really picked the right person for studies and observation collection to assist his command, Bennett had often thought.

"Ah, sir? I have the plan you requested for our approach to Alpha Post," Virgil said.

"Good. What do you get?"

"First, I think we should have our pants on and put on T-shirts with insignias in place," he started.

After a short time, the compressed undergarments were their wardrobe of choice. It did help with adapting to the heated environment.

"So, showing up half naked with no insignia might get us shot?"

"Yes, sir. If I were them, I'd be wary of anyone not bearing some military assemblage and insignias. Our hands should be off our weapons, hands up. I should be leading the team with you second and Hall last. Spacing should allow for distance in mines and grenades. I would show less deference to Hall, and she should be quiet and let us do all the talking," Virgil said.

Hall had been listening and was nodding to everything Virgil said.

"Hear that, Hall? Think you could be silent and give the impression of weakness, deference, and compliance?" Bennett said.

"Sure can," she said immediately.

Bennett had come to understand that Hall's humor was always dry and perfectly timed. Her lack of expression as the "straight man" made the humor that much more powerful. Still, he hated to play a role of superiority when, truth be told, he felt like they were all equals.

While Bennett was happy that Virgil's assessment was right on the money, and that the three days of practice of asking him to explain, plan, and strategize various suggestions while in the field was enhancing his thinking and hopefully adding to military experience, it was disheartening to know that his assessment of what they were walking into was accurate: tightly wound patrician men in a hostile environment who wanted to know they still mattered, that they were in their place, and that everyone else—slave, pleb, and surf—was in their place as well.

"Sir? Did I leave something out? Something wrong?" Virgil said.

Bennett could feel a frown on his face, his tightened jaw and fists. It was easy to see why the young lieutenant would think he was angry with him.

"No, Virgil. You're on point. It just pisses me off that we must act so differently in the presence of my class. It's, well, it just doesn't seem right," Bennett explained.

"I know, sir. It sucks," Virgil said.

"But if we don't do what's expected, and if they have no intel on our arrival—and it's not clear they do—then keeping things as they expect is critical to our survival and mission integrity," Hall said.

Bennett nodded in agreement. Virgil did the same.

"It still sucks," Bennett said.

"Yes. It still does," Virgil added.

Silence fell, and without a further word, Bennett started changing to the garb suggested and doing a weapon's check and inventory review. They were about to get ready to leave when an unmistakable howl roared in the distance behind them. It was far, but the intensity of the howl, or rather, competing howls was intimidating and was too close for comfort.

"Ah, how far are we away from Alpha?" Bennett asked.

"One and a half miles. Should we double-time it?" Virgil asked.

Both men looked at Hall: the lowest rank, not even

commissioned, and still the most well-informed, most experienced of the trio, and on things Kurtz- and Mars-related. She gave an unexpected response.

"Run. Those were at least two canines howling in close succession. They are in a pack. Sounds like they're hunting. I'd run now and slow it down once we have eyes on the outpost."

Bennett looked at her intently and then Virgil. Virgil didn't need any more explanation—he collected his gear and was ready to bolt.

"All right, run for your lives," Bennett said more to himself than the others. They were already on the move.

CHAPTER THIRTEEN

WITH ABOUT THREE hundred feet to go, right at the edge of an open, cleared field where it met the dark boundary of the mushroom forest, illuminated in the perpetual blood-red darkness, Bennett turned to face the approaching creature. Virgil and Hall were ahead, in a full sprint, putting distance between him and what was chasing them. Whether it was fatigue, age, or something else, Bennett stopped.

"Fuck this shit! This is bullshit," he said.

Bennett turned and could see the heavy trunked canopy of mushrooms parting as if giving way to a large creature. Because of the limited light, he saw shadows of the trucks moving and felt more than saw the approaching behemoth. He took a few more steps before he turned again to face the beast. He took a second to assess the distance and then dropped to his knee and got his rifle ready. Motion detector on, he waited to turn his battle rifle light on until he was ready to pull the trigger. He checked to see if there was a loaded 5.56-caliber bullet ready to go, touched the front part of his harness to make sure the three other thirty-round magazines were in place for easy access. He quickly unflapped his 10mm sidearm and ensured magazines were also available for easy access. Satisfied, he was ready for a fight. He felt he was ready to die too. It was an odd, calm feeling. It was almost as if he expected it. He chuckled at the thought that this moment might be remembered as "Bennett's Last Stand." Absent of seriousness, it made him laugh out loud.

Finally, the howling canine broke its cover. The motion detector showed the creature a mere thirty feet ahead of his position. He flicked his 2,000 lumens light on the creature and froze—the thing in front of him was a larger than expected canine beast, with a still larger than expected chest and three large heads with massive gaping jaws dripping with saliva. If there was ever a creature designed to represent a dog from hell, it was this thing. Temporarily blinded by the light, the monster stepped back, unsure where to go. It was the animal's resounding growls in stereo that jolted Bennett out of his shock.

Bennett pressed the trigger right where the light illuminated and started shooting. He felt every bullet recoil press into his shoulder. Rather than keeping it fully automatic, he kept it semiautomatic to control both the aim and ammunition expelled.

Slow, controlled bursts, he had told Virgil if it ever came to shooting. It was hard to follow his own advice. Once he completed the thought, his magazine was done, and the creature was still in play. He dropped the mag, slammed another into place, and by the time he had his weapon back on target, the three-headed dog seemed unbearably close. The motion detector had it at twenty feet. Somehow in just a few seconds, the animal recovered and was closer to its meal.

His weapon fired as quickly as he could put the trigger. The creature seemed to fall back a little, but Bennett had no idea by how much. Again, his mag went dry; he dropped the mag release, grabbed and slammed another one in, and had his rifle back on target. Again, the creature was closer, ten feet this time. He could smell its hot breath and feel the spit it threw off, or maybe it was blood. Bennett knew that this would be the last clip he could get in before the creature would be on top of him. The mag ran dry, but instead of reloading, he dropped the battle rifle with the light still on and pulled out his 10mm handgun. Compared to his rifle, the number and caliber of the handgun was about half.

"Shit," he said aloud. It was no mystery to him that he was about to die.

Whether it was divine intervention, blind luck, or the competing theory that all existence was a virtual reality, or it was just not his time to go, he saw two bright battle rifle lights focus on the creature's heads, then heard a series of 5.56 discharges ringing in his ears. His handgun ran out. He holstered it, picked up his own rifle, dropped the mag, and yelled out, "Reloading!" In seconds, he joined the shooting.

He heard Virgil yell out, "Reloading!" He and Hall were shooting. Just as Virgil started up again, he heard Hall yell out she was reloading, and a couple of seconds later, Bennett was pulling out his fifth and final magazine. Before he could say the obvious that he was reloading, the creature howled louder than Bennett thought possible. Then it crashed to the ground, adding to the constant reverberations.

The shooting stopped. He could hear magazines dropping and fresh ones being added, and then the other rifle lights joined his, remaining focused on the massive lifeless carcass just nine feet away from him. Bennett did not move. He felt spit, the creature's blood, and his own sweat drench him. He was sure he hadn't pissed himself because the amount of sweat he excreted left no more liquid left to be expelled.

He heard footsteps behind him. He presumed it was Hall and Virgil flanking him while their lights grew bigger on the dead beast. Weapons still trained on it, Hall approached one of the heads, her hand still poised on the carbine's trigger while another felt for breathing. She confirmed that it was dead. She backed away and did the same thing to the other head and said the same thing. It was only then that she relaxed her weapon as did Virgil. Bennett took a little longer to comply.

"Are you okay, sir?" Virgil asked.

Bennett took in a sharp breath, dropped his last mag, and relaxed.

"Yes," he said.

"Why did you stop and fight?" Hall asked.

"I don't know. When I get an answer, I'll tell you," Bennett said.

"I would like to hear that," another voice said close behind them.

Bennett and his teams' rifle lights were up and looking behind them. They were met by a far brighter set of lights, blinding them so that one hand had to shield their eyes while the other kept their guns up. Bennett was painfully aware that his weapon was empty.

CHAPTER FOURTEEN

"STAND DOWN, Captain Bennett. Lieutenant David Strong here, Alpha Post commander, Fort Deadly. Confirm name and purpose?"

The voice was not hostile. A surprise for Bennett. It was almost pleasant, which in a place like this, seemed strange.

"Acting Captain Willard Bennett, Lieutenant Virgil Johnson, and Specialist Betsy Ann Hall—we're all dispatched from the battle group, led by Captain T. J. Jackson Taylor on the *Robert E. Lee*," Bennett said.

"Yup, Stonewall himself. He has major cred here," Strong said. "Mission parameters?"

Bennett hesitated. With the bright lights on him, he couldn't visually confirm that they were actual patrician soldiers from the actual outpost.

"Come on, Captain, I don't need DNA on your mission parameters. Captain Taylor negotiated passage through Freeport, and he had a team arriving in three days with supplies. He told me your recon MAC–SOG team was operating in this area, which is crazy. He told me you told his XO what your mission was at his table weeks ago," the voice explained.

The flashback of the captain and XO nearly having a duel and Bennett telling the XO what his intentions were regarding Cassandra Kurtz jumped to mind. Only someone who was at that table could have told this commander what was said.

"Mission parameters are to track, find, and kill Cassandra Kurtz," Bennett said.

There was an uneasy moment of silence before Lieutenant Strong spoke again.

"Stand down, boys, we have guests tonight. And they brought us fresh decent food," Strong said in a celebratory fashion. Cheers went up, and the lights pointing at them dropped and headlamps turned on.

Lieutenant Strong and his men were all dressed in similar uniforms, but they were all in water-wicking shorts, T-shirts, and an array of clothing and gear that seemed individual for a regimented cohort. They all had shaved heads and little facial hair, most likely to keep cool. And finally, all the soldiers were armed with gas-propelled firearms of similar make and model as he and his team were using. Already, there were three men that were powering up chain saws and two others pushing large two wheeled wagons to the carcass that was about to be butchered.

Strong was leading him and his team to the outpost while the chain saws receded in the background. Other men moved to help and cover the men getting food prep together. There were still other men stationed in dugouts fifty feet away from the outpost front gate.

"That was some pretty badass shit you all did back there. We've been waiting for an opportunity to off that fucking thing, and here you all bring it to our doorstep and kill the fucker for us," Strong said.

"We aim to please," Virgil answered.

Bennett looked at him and smiled. Virgil was integrating into the fold either naturally or on purpose to get intel.

He's learning, Bennett thought.

"It's a good thing you didn't even bother with your LR-issued rifle. The energy packs deplete after three of four sustained bursts. It might be just constant heat and the weird magnetic field this place has going," Strong said.

"Good to know. Thank you," Virgil said.

"It's been a while since we had actual meat. Way better than our rations, and better than those bugs. You cook it long enough, it really starts to taste like chicken substitute of the best kind. You've made friends today," Strong said.

"Lieutenant Strong? May I ask a question?" Hall asked.

Her approach was the expected deferential approach of any plebian civilian to a patrician man.

Strong stopped and turned toward her. Bennett felt as if he might have to defend her. He saw Virgil move closer to her, as if he might have to jump in.

Wow, Virgil has changed.

"Sure, Betsy Hall," Strong said. His voice, stance, and focus on her was that of a patrician officer's presentation to a full patrician female citizen. Very unexpected here. It was confusing to Bennett. Here was an officer in a hellscape, far from civilization of Earth and even her colonies, half dressed in battle fatigue shorts and T-shirts, addressing a pleb woman as politely as possible.

"We are low on 5.56 and protein bars, and need to recharge some of our gear," she asked.

"You bet. Captain Taylor said you would need to refit and refuel before you headed out again. He also told me to tell you something like 'Use captain's discretion on when to carry on, but recommend you wait for support and supplies.' Stonewall sounds like he's a caring guy too," Strong said.

Virgil, Hall, and then Strong looked at him to see what he wanted to do. The thought of waiting was appealing. They could use the three-day rest and more support. At the same time, if "support" was XO Lee, then he would prefer to be gone with the two he knew he could count on.

"We'll refit, refuel, and rest until 08:00 tomorrow, then depart by 09:30. Thank you for your hospitality, Lieutenant," Bennett said.

"Are you kidding me? Thank you, guys. Your arrival here put us back on the map for a shitload of much needed supplies, especially with the additional men we've acquired. The *Manassas* never showed, and we just found out why. That sucked. I feel bad for cursing them," Strong said.

As they walked and talked, Bennett noticed that there were far more men in the camp than expected, with some cots outside in the open air, or rather, open cavern. The fortifications also looked to be improved, and shifted spears, barriers, and dugouts even inside the compound made the place look as if it were ready for hand-to-hand combat.

"Forays and supply runs to the other outposts yielded nothing, and that's where we would lose men," Strong continued

"Wait a minute. I don't understand. No supplies have been able to get through, but you got more men?" Virgil asked.

"No, these additional men are from the other outposts, aren't they?" Hall deduced.

"On the nose, Hall. We had five total, and now there is just us. We were all established and dug in about four years ago. It was peaceful until Echo outpost breached Mount Krakatoa over there, and then the outpost was overrun and fell under consistent attacks by small hit-and-run tactics," Strong said.

In the direction Strong pointed was the landmark to where Bennett and his team had been heading. It was the highest point in the area, a good overwatch for this dark cavern where the smallest of lights could be seen from miles away.

"We mistakenly thought that Kurtz and her troops would just take over Echo, but they stripped it of any useful things and then worked their way backward, taking out Gamma, Delta, Charlie and Bravo. All done in eighteen months. They were methodical and thorough. Stripped the outposts bare, killed anyone who fought back—and that was a lot. They've kept us bottled up right here," Strong said

The group stopped just outside of a structure that looked like sleeping quarters. Strong gestured with his head to specific locations.

"To my left is the first aid station to clean up anything opened and cut. Pick up some antibacterial tablets to last you if you think you'll be out there. We boil everything, but if you're on the move, you won't have that luxury. Right behind you are three prepped sleeping quarters. Ammo and supply depots are in three separate locations at eleven, two, and four o'clock."

The lack of pointing caught Virgil's eye. Most people would point unless they were trained not to, either because of experience or necessity.

"LT, are we being watched?" he asked.

Strong's voice dropped, his cadence and tempo slowed, and his appearance darkened to match the mood and the atmosphere that surrounded them all. He turned off his headlamp, closed the gap between them, and spoke in such a serious and grave fashion, Bennett grew nervous.

"Stay vigilant. We are always in battlefield conditions. No saluting and no pointing out resources. All the other outposts fell. The less strict and prepped, the more men lost and faster the outposts fell. I'm not going to let that happen here. Assume the enemy is watching all the time, which I am certain they are. I mean, come on—fully trained soldiers with well-armed and stocked supplies all are captured and killed within months of each other, and we didn't even find one body? They are lucky, gifted, well prepared and lethal. There are eyes everywhere," Strong said.

Bennett didn't know what to say except nod. His team did the same.

Strong took a step back, turned his headlamp back on, and spoke in a more relaxed, almost easygoing manner, much like when they'd first met.

"Dinner will be ready at 15:30 hours, so you can get your stuff stowed, supplies gathered, cleaned up, and then eat. That should give you more than enough time to get a shit ton of shut-eye before you head out tomorrow. Oh, and Captain Taylor asked that you upload your logs for review and said if Lieutenant Johnson is with you, he wants him to fall back to the ship, if you're okay with that and don't need his support," Strong said.

"I won't be doing that, sir, unless that's a direct order," Virgil said, without hesitation.

"Are you sure, Johnson? Unless you killed someone back on the ship, and even if you did, getting out of here would be the smart thing. I'm just saying," Strong said.

"Thanks, LT. I'm good," Virgil repeated.

Strong too another look at all of them and took his leave.

"See you later. You'll love how the men prep the food," Strong said.

"Thank you," Bennett and Hall said at the same time.

When there was some distance between them and Strong, Bennett made a huddle-up motion with his fingers, and they all pulled into a tight circle with lamps off. It was hard to see their faces clearly, but it would be impossible to see at a distance with the lights off.

"Well, this is all unexpected," Bennett said.

"I don't even know where to begin," Hall said.

"So, Virgil, how would you put all this together?" Bennett asked.

He took a moment to collect his thoughts before he

answered. He was getting good at summing up events, which was good practice for a sitrep and status update.

"Everything that we have experienced in the field has been accurate, including the effectiveness of firearms, the rising danger of Kurtz and her people, and her mostly likely location," he said.

"Why do laser rifles and other heavy equipment and electronics fail here?" Hall asked.

"More likely because of the persistent heat," Virgil said.

"Why not the nanite atmosphere processors?" Hall added.

"I can only guess that the interior processors are affected, but the nanites repair them quickly," he answered.

"Where do you think Kurtz base of operation is?"

"Overwatch position. High elevation, I bet. Probably right where the lieutenant thinks. She kept her location and pushed everyone back rather than forfeit an excellent position," Virgil said.

Hall and Bennett nodded in approval. Virgil was excelling in battlefield assessment.

"Should we wait until reinforcements come?" Bennett asked.

Virgil didn't answer immediately. He was clearly trying to figure out a couple of variables.

"If Kurtz holds overwatch position, it might be harder for her to see a covert, smaller group. It will be faster to travel with a small ream. Easier to infiltrate, and potentially easier to get closer to the target if secrecy is maintained. We will lose all of that if we wait three days. The enemy will also have more time to prepare and react. Also, and I don't mean to sound disrespectful, if the XO takes over field operations, I'm not, well, trusting of his approach based on his decisions at Freeport," Virgil said.

"So, we depart early tomorrow to get a jump on our arriving reinforcements and find Kurtz and tag her for elimination before it's fucked up by XO Lee. Yup. That sounds about right," Bennett said.

"Yes, sir," Virgil said.

"Agreed," Hall said.

"Well, time's wasting. Let's break, get more kit, clean up, eat, drink, and above all sleep," Bennett said, and then the team broke the huddle.

CHAPTER FIFTEEN

Bennett, Willard
    Acting Captain
    MAC–SOG
    ETZ: 07:40
    Day 4 or 5 since tunnel exit
    Hall, B.A.— Specialist
    Johnson, Virgil—LT, Robert E. Lee

Begin entry:

Lieutenant Strong was right—all the outposts were stripped of anything useful, including composite wood, metals, and plastics. Nothing was left except for foundations. What's most amazing is that all the posts—from Echo outpost sixteen miles away from Alpha to Bravo only four miles away—have been equally and completely emptied. How Kurtz and her people were able to do that so close to Alpha without arousing suspicion is impressive.

To avoid the wildlife, we travelled as close as we could to the lava vents. The lava river is the most direct route to the volcano they call Krakatoa. We moved farther away instead to a less visible but hot enough area to dissuade creatures and watch out for the curious. The closer we get to the volcano, the greater the sense that we are being watched, whether it be by two-foot animals or the native ones.

In addition to replenishing our ammunition stores, we exchanged the laser rifle for two combat axes, high-grade titanium from the recon team guys from Charlie Post relocated at Alpha. Lieutenant Strong also gave us three additional water canteens and a hydration backpack. Finding room for them meant leaving what little was in our packs, which were mostly clothes and about a quarter of the ammunition. Since water is critical and we had only one major encounter with one of those beasts, it made sense. We are prepared for a small group of insurgents, rather than the hundreds, maybe thousands that await us.

I am beginning to feel bad about Hall and Virgil. I know this is a one-way trip. Even if I do find Kurtz, we are an army of three. Of the three of us, Hall has the best chance to make it out, and Virgil might make it after six days in this hellhole. Especially if they do it soon. But me? Between incarceration, unplanned extended cryo-sleep, age, limited medical interventions, and a whole lot of wear and tear from this sojourn, I wouldn't last long in any close-quarter combat. That's why I gave my combat knife and axe to Virgil and exchanged his folding stock semiautomatic rifle for my larger one. He'll have more of a chance.

As much as I hate to admit it, the hate I had for Cassandra seems like a waste of time. I've seen only a few examples of patricians of true honor. I'm not one of them, especially when I was captain. That might have been the summit of my arrogance. How did Captain Taylor avoid being tainted by our system? How did he find the doctor and the chief? And Lieutenant Strong? I mean, he treated us all

equally, with civility and generosity in a hot zone, under fire
and contact threat of danger, and he held a feast like it was a
barbecue beach party. Hall and Virgil? They are good people.
They don't have to die.

End entry.

BENNETT TOOK A DEEP BREATH, closed his eyes, then opened them. Ever since he had been locked in the dark, hot hell, he finally figured out the trick of seeing better; closing your eyes made the ambient blackness seem less dark and foreboding. Hall mentioned it to him and Virgil once they left Alpha. At first, Bennett thought she was crazy, but after doing it a couple of times, it worked very well. Virgil did the same. and it had had a positive effect on his mood. He also was talking more freely, asking more questions, obviously trying to learn more. Bennett turned to see them both in quiet conversation. Like him, they were totally covered in dried mud, a trick they discovered to avoid the canine and felines. The mud was mere dust by now, most running off as they had ascended about three hundred feet up the volcano. It was getting hotter. He took another deep breath and decided that now was the time to break the news.

"The reason that barbecue was so good was because you were hungry. Starvation will make anything taste great," Hall said.

"I guess. Still, it did taste like chicken. Did you get a bullet? I swear I did," Virgil said.

Bennett stood there for a second, and that caught both of their attention.

"Need to huddle up, sir?" Virgil asked.

"No, this is something I've been putting off, and I hope if anyone is listening, they will hear this," Bennett said.

The puzzled look on their faces, under other

circumstances, might have been funny to see, especially Hall because she didn't do puzzled looks.

"I'm very sure that Kurtz is close, and that it's all going to end soon. Like the LT said, there are eyes everywhere. I need to go. You two have valuable human intelligence that will be vital to get back to Captain Taylor," Bennett started.

"We are close, Captain, so why stop now? With the three of us, there is a much better chance of success," Hall said.

"Yeah, a much better chance we'll all be killed. Look, this has always been a one-way ticket for me, and before, I was okay with it being a one-way ticket for you both. But that's changed. You both have a lot more to offer, and it will all be lost if you stay with me," Bennett said.

"Sorry, sir, but you're my superior officer . . ." Virgil started.

"And as your superior officer, you have new orders— escort Specialist Hall off this volcano, back to Alpha outpost to meet up with the captain. Both of you brief him on intelligence so far," Bennett said.

Both Hall and Virgil looked at him blankly.

"Come on, team, do me this one favor. If we find Kurtz, we all die, and nothing is gained. If I die and you both make it out, you will have collected valuable intelligence and gained experience few have and be able to pick up her trail sooner than later. Honestly, I can't see that wasted. I'm an old man now, and the admiralty was never going to let me live anyway. Do me this favor and live. It will help me feel better after being a less than kind man."

Bennett never felt like this before. The weight of these two subordinates possibly dying had been weighing heavily on him ever since he'd made it back to New Georgia. Five days in the dark cavern seemed like years. He couldn't bear the idea of seeing them die when they had so much more to offer in life.

"Please," Bennett said.

Both Hall and Virgil had been sitting on the ground, looking down, or at least, that's what it looked like as he finished talking. Virgil started to get up when Bennett heard something whistle by.

"Fuck! What was that?" Virgil said.

He was not fully standing when his right hand shot up to his neck where he might have been stung by some unknown insect that prowled the volcano, a danger they didn't foresee.

Virgil dropped back down, caught by Hall, and he fell back. Another whistle came in and out of his hearing range, and Hall's free left hand shot up to the left side of her throat. By that time, Bennett was moving. He heard something but couldn't make out what it was. He felt pain, two separate pain locations, both right sides, a sharp needlelike pain that stung. Bennett looked at Hall.

"Darts . . . losing consciousness," he heard her say.

Bennett took two steps forward and felt the ground rushing toward him. He really couldn't tell if he had hit the ground as his body felt enveloped by darkness. It was as if he was under anesthesia. If it weren't for the fact that that he and his team were in a danger zone, he might have enjoyed the experience.

"Fuck me," he said before the heavy weight of darkness lightened, and he felt like he was floating.

Am I dying? Bennett wondered.

CHAPTER SIXTEEN

BENNETT FELT as if he were slowly coming out of a deep sleep. He tried to roll over on his side but felt hindered, as if something was pulling at his hands. He slowly opened his eyes to discover that there was more light than he had expected. He blinked several times to clear away the cobwebs in his head, and to create some eye lubrication, as the room or wherever he was felt hot as hell.

He sat just a little longer, checked to see if there was anything broken, and then did his best to sit up. Gone were the days of jackknifing from a prone to sitting position, so he rolled to his side, which slowly compensated to allow him to sit on his butt. He looked around at what appeared to be an exceptionally large cave with torches generating light and an unbearable amount of heat in addition to the already hot underworld.

Lava flows, heat vents, and now torches were just the beginning of the heat fest; the room was filled with men and women all in a circle, all staring at him, Hall, and Virgil. They were already awake, kneeling with two large men right behind them with short swords ready to cut them down if they moved.

"Sorry I'm late to the party. Sitrep," Bennett said, hoping that some humor might lighten the mood.

"Location and time elapsed are unknown. Weapons, water, clothes, kit, and gear all gone. Surrounded by the most diverse group I have ever seen, no obvious form of rank and file. And we are captives," Virgil explained.

"So, we found them, and we have them right where we want them," Bennett said.

Surprisingly, Virgil chuckled.

Poor kid. He has no idea we're going to die, Bennett thought.

"How long was I out?" he asked.

"It could have been a day or an hour. Whatever they used, it knocked the shit out of me. I felt nothing until I woke up, and that was an hour before you, I guess," Hall said.

With his eyes adjusted, he took a long look at the people looking right back at him. There were an array of skin colors, some with differing hairstyles and hues. An even distribution of men and women were represented. One woman looked as if she was a minute away from giving birth. The majority were all half naked, mostly young, all athletic, toned. All were heavily armed with multiple weapons from firearms to edge weapons to bows and arrows and, obviously, darts. There had to be at least a hundred about two to three rows deep in an oval circle with Bennett and his crew right in the middle. For his part, he and his team were down to their compression undergarments, stripped of rank, clothes, and weapons, and bound at the wrists.

Bennett was taking it all in when he made out two shadows walking with determination toward them. Still too far away for details, it was easy to see one was a taller man and the other was a smaller woman. The woman stopped abruptly, turned to face the guy following her, and the man stopped short from bumping into her. There was some exchange of words from her to the man, and then she turned back to his direction. Her image and details were becoming clear the closer she got, but then she slowed to a stop in front of Hall and Virgil, and addressed something to the man behind her, who shook his head affirmatively. Narrowing his eyes, Bennett was pretty sure she was eyeballing Hall and not the pair or Virgil. Once again, she came back on approach.

Bennett was taking it all in when he heard the voice. It was familiar. He remembered it both from his past from the *Jefferson Davis* to intercepted radio transmissions before he'd left Earth to find her. The voice was clear, strong, and animated. What was easy to discern was that the owner of the female voice lacked all insecurities. Not exactly hubris, but more playfulness in a situation Bennett only could describe as dire for him and his crew. He looked in the direction of the voice to see Cassandra Kurtz—a now bald head, smaller than most, clad in her own compression garments, and armed with curved knives on her belt in addition to two semiautomatic sidearms and a large semiautomatic rifle stowed on her back. For a small woman, she carried a lot of weapons. It was hard to believe she was once part of Earth's ruling class that promoted femininity and motherhood.

"Captain Willard Bennett. It has been too long. I hear you've been assigned to kill me. How is that working out for you?" Kurtz said.

She walked right up to him without reservation and hesitation. To her right was Bennett's former ship's doctor, Thomas, who abandoned his post and left with her. At the time, Bennett hated him for that but after his time at Delta Exchange, he thoroughly understood why the man left Earth and his commission behind. Oddly, he had more clothes on than the rest. He looked thinner and darker since the last time they'd seen each other. In the here and now, Bennett was caught off guard that he would find his former colleague. A feeling of remorse kicked in, and he did his best not to be a dick to him like he had been the last time.

"You're part of a new task force: Military Assistance Command–Studies and Observation Group. A task force developed in 1964 for a conflict the former United States had with a Southeast Asian country called Vietnam. Looks like your Captain Taylor has revived an old strategy to deal with a similar old foe. Things haven't changed on Earth. It's still reviving old ideas and strategies, you know, like slavery," Kurtz said.

Bennett's expression clearly reflected how she had already known so much about what was going on when he'd had no idea about what MAC–SOG was up to until a week or so ago.

"I have a highly active AI up here. Aletheia says hello, by the way. She can pull up history, the real stuff, like no other," Kurtz said.

"Okay," was all Bennett could say. He turned his attention to his former doctor.

"Lieutenant Thomas. I never thought I would say this, but I'm glad you're alive," Bennett said.

"Me too," Thomas said.

The exchange felt genuine, which was odd, as Bennett was so focused on Kurtz that he forgot the doctor's desertion. Still, he had no ill feelings about it, and he was not sure why. Maybe it was the passage of time. Maybe the trek and hardships from prison to hell. Either way, he was not feeling the expected animosity he thought he should have toward the traitor.

"You look good," Bennett said. He actually meant it; the doctor was lean, fit, dressed in more clothes but enough to show his arms, legs, and neck had no fat.

"Thank you. I hate to say it captain, but you've looked better," the doctor said.

"No offense taken. I've been better. It's an off day," Bennett explained.

Bennett took a deep breath and turned his attention to Cassandra Kurtz.

"Well, Cassandra IX, former patrician and first-class citizen, now identified as Cassandra Kurtz—you are charged with terrorism and being the architect of a war directed at the established world order," Bennett announced.

Kurtz gave the impression she was taking the charge seriously, even though Bennett himself felt that the accusations were hollow since he was sure they were going to die.

"All true except the last part. One person's traitor is another person's freedom fighter. And for me, Mars is a new planet, and the new order will be that all people are equal. Earth's class system is no longer viable on this planet," she said.

"All right. Does a dying man have one request in your world order?" Bennett asked.

He was surprised that Kurtz was herself surprised. She took a step back, not out of fear but to take a better look at him.

"So, no grandstanding and debating the virtues of the Third Republic," she asked.

Bennett sighed and slowly shook his head no.

"Nope. You got me. You win," he said.

There was no sarcasm, no hubris, and no attitude. For Bennett, his desire to kill Kurtz was left on Earth, on the ride home from the Delta Exchange. Now all he wanted to do was to keep his team, his friends, alive.

Kurtz placed her hands on her hips. And looked like she was thinking. Then she folded her arms and asked a question.

"And that would a condemned man want?"

"Let my team go. Their biggest mistake is being loyal to

me. I was sending them back when you captured us. It's my only request. You can do with me what you want," Bennett explained.

"I can do that anyway," she said.

"I know. That's why I am asking you to do this. Please," he said.

Kurtz was quiet again, clearly deep in thought or listening to the AI implant. Bennett took a chance and addressed his former doctor in the hopes their history, as difficult as it had become, might prevail and allow mercy for Hall and Virgil.

"Please, Thomas. I'm dead. I accept that. But these two have done nothing wrong. Hall is a pleb, and Virgil is just a kid, really," Bennett said.

A chorus of objections erupted from Hall and Virgil, denying what he was saying and objecting to the proposal.

"Silence! I want to hear him out," Kurtz said.

The command worked. There was no mistaking it. This woman had changed.

Without much fanfare, Kurtz pulled out the computer tablet where all the logs were kept. Facial and fingerprint locked, it was obvious she had secured both while he was asleep.

"I have to say, Captain, that you surprised me. When I heard you were at the front door at Freeport, and you all were acting like dicks, I thought you were the main asshole. Come to find out, you were the voice of reason," she said.

"No one's perfect. Please, can we focus on the here and now? Do we have a deal?" Bennett pressed.

Kurtz ignored his question and continued to speak to him.

"And then, you retrace my escape route and make every effort to find me, staying on task, which is expected. But what was not expected is that there is no clear rank or order in your task force. You patricians like rank and order, especially since you're all on top," Kurtz said.

"*We* patricians, Cassandra," Bennett corrected. "You were a full-fledged patrician, a first-class citizen once."

"I know, and I can see the difference in how you treated those two and how they would have been treated by a regular patrician," she said.

Bennett was trying to think of something that might work. It was hard to listen to her and think of an escape plan at the same time.

"Sharing water, giving advice to a junior officer, listening to a female nonpatrician specialist with a prosthetic leg, who really does know what she's doing, and all of these behaviors are different from what one would expect from a patrician officer."

For the first time, Bennett was shocked. He knew he wasn't a special-ops soldier, but he wasn't ignorant.

"Wait, you been that close to us all that time?" Bennett asked.

"No. That's not possible . . . how could you have done that?" Hall said.

The pain on Hall's face, crestfallen, was hard to see, but it was there. Bennett could see it, distinguish it from her typical stoic expression.

"You're good, Hall, incredibly good. The Captain Willard Bennett I knew would have left you to die once he was free of the tunnels, so your being alive, getting far as you did, is, well, amazing," Kurtz said.

"Unbelievable," Virgil chimed in.

Kurtz shifted her attention to Virgil. Bennett saw that she took out a serrated curved knife and kept it concealed, as if she planned to get close to Virgil and cut his throat.

Bennett made a desperate attempt to tell Virgil not to talk when one of Kurtz's guards placed their blades against

Bennett's own throat, rendering him silent and unable to move.

"And you are?" she said to Virgil.

Virgil shifted his posture so he was kneeling erect with his head up high and stared straight ahead, standard approach when you are sure you will be integrated or worse.

"Lieutenant Virgil Johnson from the warship *Robert E. Lee*, temporarily assigned to Captain Bennett," he said.

"How long have you've been with Captain Bennett?"

"Five or six days on ground, one day in orbit," Virgil said.

Strictly speaking, Virgil had given their captors too much information, though it was far from vital.

Forced to stare ahead and watch the interaction, Bennett was surprised that while Kurtz spoke to Virgil, she had been scrutinizing Hall, who continued to look down.

"Okay, Johnson. And who are you?" Kurtz asked Hall.

Her full attention was on Hall now. She was closer to her, and it looked like her knife was at the ready.

What the fuck is going on? Bennett thought.

"Betsy Ann Hall, specialist, assigned per request of Captain Taylor of the *Robert E. Lee*. Reassigned to Captain Bennett just prior to the drop to Freeport and entering the cavern system," she said.

"What happened to your leg?" Kurtz asked.

It was the first time Bennett had ever seen Hall surprised. She shifted her stare to look right at Kurtz, and then she dropped it once she saw that Kurtz was looking directly at her.

"That's classified," Hall said.

"Was it in service of the Patrician Admiralty or Tribunal?" she asked.

"No. Prior," Hall blurted out.

"If I gave you chance to leave these two behind, especially your acting captain, would you walk away?

Would you like to kill them? I mean, if you're not a patrician, you are less than, when it is obvious you are more than these two combined," Kurtz said.

Bennett was struck by Kurtz's softer tone and demeanor toward Hall.

"No. Why would I do that? They have treated me with respect and honor and as an . . ." Hall stopped her response as if she were looking for a word. It was taking her longer than Kurtz liked.

"Treated you like an equal? Was that the word? Equal," Kurtz said.

Hall decided to stay silent. Bennett was appreciative of this, as he had no idea where Kurtz was going with things. The longer she went on, the longer he had a chance to get Hall and Virgil out alive.

"Huh . . . treating a nonpatrician woman and a junior officer as equals. Equals? Not exactly the captain I remember," Kurtz said.

She was moving back to address Bennett now. The two guards retracted their knives from his throat. He felt a sting of cuts from the well-sharpened blades and a tiny trickle of blood.

Kurtz's voice went back to sounding stronger, almost imperial, projecting for everyone to hear.

"And then there's that skirmish at Alpha Post with Cerberus, our hound from Hell, that you defied and attacked to protect these two," Kurtz said, motioning her head in Hall's and Virgil's direction.

"Yet another anomaly—a patrician putting himself in danger to save a culturally diverse woman and a junior officer. She describes you and her as 'equal.' And then there's the business of their response, where they could have found safety and left you behind but instead, they came back to help you, a team effort," she said.

There was a moment of silence. Bennett forced himself to be quiet.

The longer she talks, maybe she will let them go, he thought.

Kurtz took the tablet where she had obviously been reading his logs and waved it at him to make her point. She was kneeling at his eye level and lowered her voice as if to have a more private conversation.

"I always watch for behaviors to see what people are really thinking and feeling. Behaviors seldom lie, and they most often express the truth. Add your log to the mix—such entries as, 'I am beginning to feel bad about Hall and Virgil. I know this is a one-way trip. Even if I do find Kurtz, we are an army of three,' and 'I've seen only a few examples of patricians of true honor. I'm not one of them, especially when I was captain.' And then there's this big one: 'Hall and Virgil? They are good people. They don't have to die.' Honestly, these behaviors and writings do not sound like the conniving, greedy captain of the *Jefferson Davis* I met seven-plus years ago. Self-reflection? Putting the safety of others ahead of yourself? Recognizing character flaws? Recognizing honor and respect? This Captain Bennett is someone I'd like to meet. Care to explain?" Kurtz asked.

Bennett remained silent. He felt exposed and vulnerable. He knew that someone would read his log, maybe Captain Taylor. He was also positive that he was going to be dead, and therefore, missed the part about feeling embarrassed. Worst of all, Kurtz saw how he had changed, and everyone now knew it.

"Look, I have nothing to offer you but my life. Interrogate me. Torture me. Kill me. Whatever. But killing them does nothing but waste life. You have all the intel you need. Those two are not a threat to you. Maybe Hall can join your team? She's part pleb," Bennett offered.

"Stop it. I can speak for myself," Hall said.

"I'm sorry, but . . ." Bennett started but was cut off by Kurtz.

"See? You did it again. You're making excuses to protect them. You are desperate to save them. What happened to you?"

Bennett remained silent. He had played all his cards, and it was out of his control.

Kurtz was staring at him. Waiting for an answer he really could give her. Time ticked by slowly. She waited. More silence followed. Bennett tried to think of something but was coming up with only small talk. He was tired and totally soaked from the heat and the pressure. His skin was slippery, his throat was dry, and his eyes felt like sandpaper.

Finally, he spoke. He motioned his head for her to come closer.

She kept her curved knife from her left side, and a needle appeared in her right hand. She came within whispering distance, kneeling on one knee, prepared to slit his throat if he did something stupid. He was surprised that his guards were not fully restraining him with knives at his throat again.

Bennett made sure to say as few words as possible, and as low as possible in case he triggered a rageful outburst. Hopefully, if she was sure no one heard what could be described as her weakness, a trauma that tipped the balance, she might not kill Hall and Virgil in a fury.

"I saw what an eleven-year-old patrician girl saw, lost for a half hour in a cesspool called Delta Exchange. I've seen the horror you've seen. I've seen what powerful people do to others without consequences. Without limitation, checks, and balances. I saw the reasons why you were right to change, and the inequities. And I know there's nothing I can say that will make amends, but I am sorry, and I am pleading with you to be better than me and others like me," Bennett said.

Kurtz stared deep into his eyes. They were still a deep blue, with a flickering of red from the torches' flame dancing on her irises. Expressionless, motionless, her eyes penetrated his.

"I really wish you made this easier for me," Kurtz whispered.

He felt another prick in his neck, same as before, when the two darts got him the first time. His head shot up from the pain, and then he felt immediately dizzy and lightheaded. He looked at Kurtz as she blurred out of focus.

"Ah, damn it," he said before he was out again.

PART 5

"I can't imagine what a lifetime of being told what to do, where to go, who I was, and to live or die at the whim of another could drive me to do."

CHAPTER SEVENTEEN

DARKNESS STARTED TO RECEDE, and again Bennett felt as if he was waking from a deep sleep. It felt like a very deep sleep, even deeper than when he would prep for cryo-sleep or medical procedures, though if there was a close comparison, it would be like he was put under for a major operation. He remembered that from childhood when he'd had a terrible fall and broken his leg.

That was painful, he thought.

He could tell he was breathing, and the familiar Martian cavern heat was coming to life. He had a headache, and his right hand hurt like a son of a bitch. He moved his fingers, but there was no relief.

"Hey, Captain, you coming back? No sudden movements. Adjust to your body," Hall said.

Her voice sounded softer than usual. Kinder. This was not to say she wasn't kind. Her voice was typically a matter-of-fact, reflecting a stoic outlook on life, which seemed like the most effective way to go through life, especially if you were not a patrician.

Suddenly, Bennett remembered his meeting with Kurtz.

His former doctor was there, along with Hall and Virgil as prisoners, and they were surrounded by combatants.

Bennett tried to sit up quickly but was hindered by Hall and another hand on each shoulder keeping him at bay.

"Slowly, Captain," Virgil said. "No need to break records getting up."

Bennett settled back down, feeling better knowing that Hall and Virgil were still alive.

Apparently, he was too, and it was confusing. The lighting was low, and it was obvious they were outside the cave, since it was no longer bright with torchlight and cooler. But the cavern itself seemed darker, not as clear or as bright as he remembered.

"Thirsty," Bennett said.

He was hoping that he was just dehydrated, and water would help with the dull ache in his head.

"I got it," Virgil said.

When Bennett went to grab the canteen to drink, Hall intercepted and said she would do it.

"I got it, Captain. Put your hands down and let me help," she said.

The tone was more of an order than a gentle nurse.

Bennett sat up to lean on his elbows and let Hall pour. His right hand was killing him, and his headache was still making itself known. The amount of energy he expended was far more than expected, and he thought that maybe Hall was right to hold the water.

The water was warm, but it helped soothe his throat. It was dryer than usual. A byproduct of the dart they kept jabbing him with.

Bennett pulled away and slowly lay back down. He heard plastic crinkling under him, indicating he was lying on a tarp. He coughed, cleared his throat, and then focused on his first question.

"Status report," Bennett said.

He was opening and closing his eyes to see why his vision was more monocle than binocular. His left eye felt good, but the right side was covered. There was hesitation before Hall spoke.

"You've been out for at least eight hours. When Kurtz put you out, she immediately removed you for at least two of those hours. The guards took us right here, where you are now," she said.

What the hell is wrong with her? She's almost quiet, he thought.

Bennett moved his right hand to touch his right eye. For some reason, he felt a pulsating, achy pain in the hand and couldn't feel his eye, or anything for that matter, just sharp, throbbing pain. It was only when he moved his left hand to his right eye that he discovered it was bandaged.

"What the fuck happened to me?" Bennett said.

He felt his heart rate tick up, his stomach drop, his breathing increase, and sudden stress.

"Did they torture me or something? I don't remember if they did," he explained.

He was feeling very confused. He had no memory of what happened since passing out from that second dart. If they had tortured him, he had no memory, which, when he thought about it, wasn't a terrible thing, he guessed.

Hall's changed tone and volume pulled him back to reality, moving from a caring, kind, almost gentle voice to her regular objective, clinical tone.

"Captain, I'm going to show you what happened with my headlamp. Listen to me first. I am going to tell you what they did; then I'm going to show you. Do you understand?" she said.

Bennett delayed his response to process the severity of what she said.

What they did? Shit! Not good, he thought.

"It's bad, isn't it?" he said.

Fuck! They cut my hand off or something. Fuck! Shit!

More time passed. Bennett focused on calming his breathing first, and then focused on his limbs. He felt three out of four limbs moving. He felt a wave of trepidation and dread wash over him before he spoke.

"Okay. Let me have it," he said.

Without hesitation, Hall leaped into briefing mode. She spoke of his situation just like she did when he first met her on the *Lee* when she presented her intel and findings.

"Your right eye has been removed. While I am not sure, I believe Doctor Thomas removed your optic nerve. Additionally, he removed your right hand. That is why you might be feeling pain. They are phantom pains, and they will subside over time," Hall said.

Hall then directed her headlamp light to fall in proximity of his right arm and wrist, and then she moved his left hand to his right eye where he now felt bandaged.

Bennett took a minute to process the verbal and visual information he had just received. "Fuck me," he said.

"There is also a surgical cut and treated wound on your left cheek. I have no idea what that is about other than it be a mark to remember your meeting with Kurtz," Hall said.

Bennett let out a short laugh. Whether it was shock, anxiety, or just a reaction to difficult news, he thought the idea of a scar to "remember" their meeting was funny in that he was without a right eye and a hand.

"I would think taking my hand and my eye would be a good reminder," he explained.

Bennett couldn't see her face well, but he thought she seemed less clinical. Virgil gave out a short, nervous chuckle.

"I can only guess that her taking your eye and hand has more to do with gaining control to most of our ship's access points and some controls. That makes the most sense to me. Before she left with all her crew, she wanted me to tell you a couple of things," Hall said.

As Hall spoke, he found himself looking where his hand used to be, and then feeling the bandage over his eye. He was still listening, but his distraction caused Hall to stop to obviously give him time to refocus.

"She wanted me to know a couple of things. Go. What were they?" he asked.

"First, she said the only reason you're alive is because she thinks you've changed. She said she wished you were the 'old Bennett' because she wanted to just kill you and us and be done with it," she said.

"Okay. What else?" Bennett said.

"To be clear, she was going to kill you and Virgil outright and give me a choice to stay or go, but I guess you changed her mind," she said.

"Got you. What else?" he asked.

"She said that she took what she 'needed from you' and left you a scar 'to mark the occasion.' And she said something I don't understand, unless there is a specific meaning other than what I've seen in old naval documents," she said.

Bennett nodded.

"Let's have it. I'm sure it's something prophetic," Bennett said.

"She said, 'Unfurl the skull and crossbones, raise the black flag, and fuck the patriarch,'" Hall said.

It took Bennett a minute to absorb the words. If there was any hidden meaning in the use of a famous pirate flag and high seas slogan about thieves, outlaws and legitimate ships, he was missing it.

"Well, Captain? What do you think?" Virgil asked.

"I think Kurtz says what she means. I think she's saying I should go independent and keep away from the admiralty and probably the patricians. I don't think there's any hidden message or riddle. If anything, Kurtz has been direct in all her moves," Bennett said.

He motioned his right handless arm to his right bandaged eye.

"Kind of a case in point in saying what she means and doing what she says," he said.

"I agree, sir. And with that, I think she intends to steal a shuttle, board the *Lee*, and make things go sideways," Hall said.

"Hence, my hand and eye. We've got to move out. Did she leave us anything?" Bennett asked.

Virgil gave the inventory. There was something about his voice that seemed different. Less anxious, more secure. *Confident?*

"She left us all our water and then some, our purification tablets, and told us where to find all our weapons and ammo, which was right where she said it would be. She put them about ninety minutes away. I had to make two trips to get them all back, effectively keeping us at bay for more than three hours," he said.

"So, she wants us to live and make it back to the outpost," Bennett surmised.

"It's what she didn't leave us that worries me," Hall said.

"Let me guess—no shortwave radio or the tablet. We can't contact Alpha outpost to warn Captain Taylor, and taking the tablet is not just removing another way to communicate directly with the ship if we got to the surface, but it has intel on it. How much?" Bennett asked.

"Nothing she doesn't already know. All the data was focused on the ground mission and recording, with reports attached to this mission only. There are no ship schematics, data, or other mission objectives, past or present," Hall said.

"Okay," Bennett said.

"And she let us keep our dog-tag recorders. I'm sure she knows what they are," Hall said.

"That's good news, at least. And I guess she could have just killed us all. She is not what I expected," Virgil said.

"No, she is not. She's changed in so many ways, but that's not important right now. We've got to move," Bennett said as he tried to stand. Hall's and Virgil's assistance was necessary. Even if he had both hands, getting up off the tarp on the ground was difficult for him on a good day.

"As much as I would like to argue the points and stay and have you properly recover, I agree," Hall said.

"Once we get close enough, I might be able to double-time it to the base," Virgil offered.

"Okay. We'll assess as we go. Time to go," Bennett said.

He stood up and waited for the lightheadedness to leave, trying his best to adjust to one eye. Hall clearly noticed.

"It's going to take time for you to adjust to using one eye, especially in this darkness. It will be a lot easier once we're topside, and there is more light available for your left eye to use," Hall said.

Some of her kind tone had returned as she spoke. Bennett felt mixed about it. On the one hand, he liked it, as she was calming. On the other hand, he was sure she only used it when things were bad.

"Well, I'll take it slow," Bennett said.

"Okay. Let's move out," Hall said.

CHAPTER EIGHTEEN

"SO, I was thinking, unless admiralty is willing to grow you another hand, you might want to consider a hook, the type that has two pincers at the end that have a slight curve to them," Hall said from her crouched position.

She had the right forty-five-degree field of fire, and Bennett, positioned right next to her, held the left forty-five-degree field. So far, the defensive position had been working well for the last three hours since their arrival. The two hours before was more of a start-stop-shoot-dash, until they'd found the base of this massive boulder. With their backs against a wall, and some large stones in front providing limited cover, the height of the stones provided a natural shelf to place his ammunition magazines, knife, water, and combat axe. If they were being hunted by humans with guns, they wouldn't last long. But for an animal, there was hope.

Bennett was using the folding stock firearm that actually had a brace on it, which made things extremely easy for him to shoot. However, the ammo was 10mm, and not as effective as 5.56-caliber.

"You're optimistic. You think we're going to get out of this one?"

"We got one cat already, so we're fifty percent done," Hall answered.

"Keeping positive can be the difference between life and death," she added.

Bennett never thought for one second that his end would be in the form of a six-legged, ten-foot-long, genetically altered feline with a prehensile tail. He was sure he was going to be killed by Kurtz or one of her terrorists. On better days, he thought he could have gotten a sniper shot at her, or be the last man standing in a firefight, or most likely captured, like he had been, and then receive a summary execution. But no. So now, the idea of being consumed by a pair of feline monsters seemed less impressive.

Still, whether Hall was trying to change the mood or distract him from the imminent danger at hand, it worked. Prior to the decision to have Virgil break rank and sprint ahead to get help, he had been thinking about limb and eye replacements.

"You know, there's no way I'll be getting a biologically grown anything from Earth. Maybe if I had actually killed Kurtz, packed her head and hands in a box for verification and display in the naval academy square, there might have been a chance. Still, didn't you decrypt that I was going to get fragged by my own troops?" Bennett said.

"Yup. Ergo my suggestion of a pincher hook prosthetic. Also, it's easy to learn, few moving parts, easy maintenance," Hall said without hesitation.

"I am assuming you know this from experience," Bennett said.

"You meet a lot of mixed breeds, plebs, and surfers who have lost limbs. When you spend time with them, you get to know that aesthetics are a pain in the ass in costs, maintenance, and upkeep. Simple is cheaper, stronger, longer, and fixable. I'm just saying," Hall said.

"And my eye?" he asked.

"An eye patch. If you were a young man still interested in having sex, I would get the best artificial one possible, less for sight and more for aesthetics," Hall said.

"So, as an old man, most likely on Earth's hit list, a patch should do," Bennett said.

"That's right. Also, for us mature people interested in science, adventure, and excitement, the eye patch brings imagination. I mean, honestly, once we kill this thing, I could go for a hot bath, warm wine, and three days of sleep. After that, if I can, I'll be staying on this rock to do field studies on the fauna, flora, and monsters," Hall said.

As she spoke, he could hear excitement and even joy in her voice. It was easy to comprehend that her being on Mars, and away from Earth and officers, meant she would be free.

"'Better to reign in Hell,'" Bennett quipped.

The two fell silent. Bennett was doing his best to listen for any movement. That's how they got the one feline. With eyesight reduced to half, he had to use his bandaged right arm to wipe sweat away. After some period, Bennett started up again.

"'Mature people like us?' Aren't you, like, twenty-nine or thirty? Not exactly midfifties like me," he said.

"Since we might die, the truth is I think I turned twenty-six last week. Hard to remember the days down here," Hall said.

"Happy belated birthday. That's fucking young," Bennett said.

His right arm was tiring faster than he liked, and he needed conversation to keep him focused.

"So, what was that you told Virgil about running ahead of us to get help?" he asked.

"'Down to Gehenna or up to the Throne, he travels the

fastest who travels alone.' An ancient document written by Rudyard Kipling. One of the best things about being on Earth's surface is you find a lot of stuff that is just gone now, nowhere to be found except in the wild," Hall said.

"You should be careful whom you tell about those things. Cassandra Kurtz was caught, tried, and convicted because she found old-world documents, things about freedom and equality that got her imprisoned," Bennett halfheartedly warned.

"Huh. So that's what they got her on? At her trial, there was no mention of what she was distributing. How do you know this?" Hall asked.

"I saw all the classified data on her case before departure as a way of 'learning about the terrorist's motivation and weaknesses.' The judges and admiralty believed me. I saw more than I ever wanted to learn. I guess since I was going to be killed, it didn't matter if I saw everything," he said.

A larger than expected tremor rumbled under their feet. The reverberation felt somehow deeper than normal.

"That's odd. Have you felt anything like that before?" Hall asked.

Before he had time to answer, a violent quake erupted beneath their feet. Being in the kneeling position behind rocks with their backs against a boulder were the only things that kept them upright. The quake seemed like it was leveling out when a blast of heated air, a bona fide gust of wind, pushed the heat through, giving Bennett a sense of what the old convection ovens used to do to cook meat. Still shaken by the quake and then the blast of air, the cat they had been looking for fell from above their position. It first landed with a thud on its rear quarters, then quickly recovered on all its legs and hissed at them with large fangs.

"Motherfucker! You were waiting above us," Hall yelled out.

Hall unleashed a hail of bullets at the creature's head, as

did Bennett. His firearm only had half a magazine, so he used one hand to drop the magazine once empty, pulled out another and slammed it in, then charged the firearm to shoot when Hall ran out.

"Changing mag!" she yelled.

Bennett spaced out his twenty shots at the softer parts of the creature such as eyes, nose, and mouth. The larger caliber hurt the creature, and it looked away. When the shooting stopped, it looked back to attack but was now being pelted with a smaller caliber. It was obviously in pain as it tried to claw at their position. As soon as Hall was back up, she began shooting again, and Bennett dropped down to recycle a fresh mag, the last one left.

Fortunately, the creature hissed again, jumped back on its hind legs, hissed one more time, and then bolted away. With sweat pouring down his head and back, Bennett felt his "good" eye stinging and his right arm just under the wrist shooting with pain again.

Hall and Bennett swept their own fields of fire. Once Bennett was convinced they were clear, he crouched back down, back against the wall, and waited.

"What do you think happened? I mean, I never felt a quake like that before, and never wind. You'd think it would have been slightly refreshing, but I swear it made the heat worse," Bennett said.

"Like a convection oven," Hall said.

"That's exactly what I was thinking! You're too young to have seen one for real," Bennett said.

"We found some old mechanical stuff maybe ten years ago, including a stove. The real problem was finding the amperes to run the thing, but when we did, it kept going for an hour until it shorted out. When you opened the door, a heat wave leaped out," Hall said.

"You were out on the surface at sixteen? We're you ever confused for a surfer?" Bennett asked.

"I knew two surfer families that lived in tunnels. They were the absolute best to scavenge and trade with. My group was always on the move, and when we would hit the ports, we would make deals for them and bring back what they needed," she said.

As she spoke, she almost looked wistful, as if it was a positive childhood memory.

Silence fell again between them. Bennett was trying to remain as vigilant as Hall, but he was feeling exhausted. Waiting for help was something he was not used to doing.

"Did you ever exchange goods at the Delta Exchange?" Bennett asked.

Hall shook her head no vigorously.

"Those exchanges were slave ports, with sex trafficking of minors. Nothing good comes from there if you're a nonpatrician. That's a place I'd burn to the ground if I could, but they have a way of multiplying," she said.

Bennett could feel her disgust and anger, so he changed the subject.

"You don't think that creature got Virgil first, do you?" he asked.

Hall took a moment to process the question. It was easy to see that even when scanning the environment, she could use logic to figure out questions solely driven out of anxiety.

"No. I think those cats are opportunistic. They wait for the weak and injured to show up. If we had stayed together, they might have attacked eventually, but I think once they saw him take off, and saw us limping along, they decided on us. I think getting the first cat was easy because it got lazy. The second one was smart. I mean, I never thought to look up," she said.

"Me neither. You think they're that smart? I guess it would be a DNA code for a predator to know," Bennett said.

"Oh, I'm positive. I've seen this more often than I would like back on Earth, outside the wall. Wolves, coyotes, wild dogs and cats, things called bears, but not a lot of those, and then there are these things called rats—now, they really suck and are smart. I've seen all of them take their time, wait, watch, identify the weak, and then attack. These things are no different. Well, except for the extra pair of legs, more deadweight tonnage, and massive size," Hall said.

"It's nimble, though. Quiet too. And it had just one head," Bennett said.

Hall's attention was grabbed to the midline of their field of fire, and Bennett was positive he heard something approaching.

"Identify!" Hall called out.

"Friendlies coming in on your ten and two! Friendlies coming in on your ten and two. It's me, Virgil with LT and Alpha," Virgil said.

A huge sigh of relief let out of both. Two groups of well-armed, half-naked men broke cover and approached their position from the flanks. There were twelve total, and they set up a defensive circle that allowed Virgil and Lieutenant Strong to enter.

Without hesitation, Hall walked up to Virgil and hugged him. At first, he was confused, as was Bennett. This expression of emotion was unprecedented for Hall. To Virgil's credit, he let her hug him and hugged her back until she pulled away and retreated to pack her weapons. No one said anything about the hug and seemed to pretend as if it never happened.

"Okay. Well, it looks like you bagged a cat. Everett, Peterson, and Barrett—get its teeth, claws, eyes, and organs. Forget the rest. Take the tail too, in case we can do something with that. Davis, you stay behind with them and get them back," Strong said.

A chorus of "Yes, sir" sounded off, and Strong came closer to Bennett to size him up.

"Fuck me. You know you three are the only people to

have met with Kurtz and live to tell the tale? Still, with respect, you look like shit and probably feel just as bad," Strong said.

"You have no idea," Bennett said.

"Corpsmen! He's going to need a litter and drip, I bet," Strong said.

"On it, sir," two men said in unison.

Before he knew it, two men were placing Bennett in a makeshift litter tilted for him to lean on with two large wheels and an extension for an IV. For a homemade two-wheeled gurney, it wasn't bad at all.

Another litter, this one larger with four wheels, was pulled up by another soldier for the cat parts Strong wanted. It was easy to see that the creatures' remains were just as important as him.

"Are you going to take any of the meat?" Virgil asked.

"Nope. These creatures' meat is tough as leather and gamey. The internal organs are good for broth and fertilizer. The claws and teeth make for good edge weapons and traps, and the eyes have medicinal properties. We leave the rest for the other creatures to feast and to leave us alone," Strong explained.

"LT? Any idea what that large quake and wind was about? Have you ever experienced anything like that before?" Hall asked.

"Nope. We think that was a human-caused event. Last check in ten minutes ago indicated that the garrison, Fort Sumter, was under attack. We haven't heard anything since then but static. After that, we felt the quake and wind. I'm guessing some explosion. Massive," Strong reported.

"Kurtz? I mean, that kind of blast to level a garrison would be massive, almost nuclear. She didn't look like she and her crew were carrying anything that big," Virgil said.

Bennett was settling into his litter when he was taken by Hall's expression. It was an expression of understanding and horror at the same time. She looked up at him, and their eyes met. He looked at his right arm where his hand used to be. He flashed back to Hall's thoughts on why they would take his optic nerve and hand.

To access some access ports, minor controls, and possible shuttle crafts, he thought.

"Kurtz and her crew dug underground and into Echo and Delta outposts. There were some cave-ins, but I don't remember any explosions were used at all, let alone something that big," Strong was saying.

"LT, can you contact Captain Taylor with that shortwave radio?" Hall asked.

"No way. Not enough power," he said.

"When was the last time you talked to the captain?" Bennett asked.

"We contacted him right when Virgil arrived. He wanted to let him know what happened to you all, and about Kurtz," Strong said.

"Did you tell him about her taking my eye and hand?" Bennett asked Virgil directly.

"Yes, sir. It was brief, but I told him Hall's theory about accessing the ship with them," Virgil said.

Hall visibly relaxed. Bennett felt his chest untighten and jaw release.

Strong spoke next. It was apparent he'd figured out what the meaning of a missing eye and hand might mean for sabotage and hijacking.

"Captain Taylor was informed of the danger, but it might have been too late. He was telling me that he'd lost contact with one of his escort ships, the *Raleigh*. They were complaining about power flux and two magnetic seal breaks before they went dark about an hour before. Just before we contacted him with Virgil's news, he was at combat alert and approaching the other escort ship, the *Virginia*, because it was, well, he said, 'acting weird,' and not responding to comms either, and its orbit was shallow. He was on a dead run to get to it," Strong added.

Bennett shot a look at Hall. Before he could ask the question, she was answering.

"The admiralty would have let you have access to some of the *Manassas'* command centers, but not the *Lee*'s. She's a battle cruiser with a lot of firepower. I don't know if that means you would have access to either the *Raleigh* or *Virginia*. They are comparable to the *Manassas*. But if you did have that authority, accessing a shuttle or two, entering one of the ships . . ." she said.

"Captain Taylor and the chief told me those ships were bottom heavy with slaves, surfers, and plebs. Only patrician officers and some junior officers," Virgil added.

"All they need is a shuttle to board a ship. Offer everyone freedom. Seize that ship with minimal resistance. Crash it into the garrison," Bennett said.

"Whoa. That would mean killing everyone on board. I can't say for certain, but I might be okay where I was than to die in a blaze of glory," Strong said.

A sudden wave of anger came over Bennett. It was so easy to see why someone would willingly die to kill others.

"I was in prison for only eighteen months, a drop in the ocean in comparison compared to servitude and slavery, and I would have considered death to get revenge. I can't imagine what a lifetime of being told what to do, where to go, who I was, and to live or die at the whim of another could drive me to do. All that, and I'm given a chance to end it all and to take as many fuckers as possible with me? I'd do it in a heartbeat," Bennett said.

"Well, yeah. I'd probably feel the same way," Virgil said.

"Nope. No one other than the patrician officers are going to die. They boarded the *Raleigh* first, hijacked it, then boarded the *Virginia* and used that ship as a weapon of mass destruction. Kill the garrison, cut off patrician command, steal a ship, build up your troops, and leave no bodies behind," Hall said.

"Fuck me. She's fucking brilliant. Shit," Strong said.

Another tremor, not as violent as the first one but more than the usual volcanic reverberations, shook under their feet.

"We got to move," Bennett said.

He suddenly felt his leaning position fall into a prone position and the ride begin.

"Davis—you and your team pick up the pace and double-time it back. Don't take too long," he heard Strong say.

"They crashed the *Virginia* and stole the *Raleigh*. They destroyed the garrison, and now they have a ship. The admiralty is going to be pissed," Hall said.

Bennett felt bad that he was being driven back to safety while everyone was carrying their own things and now him too. It didn't seem fair, he thought. On that note, he was positive he was going to be blamed for everything else too, in addition to not killing Kurtz. He was in deep thought and then chuckled at what Hall had said earlier.

"You know, Hall, I don't think I'll be getting either my hand or my eye grown," Bennett said.

"No, sir. I don't think you or I should go anywhere near Earth," Hall said.

CHAPTER NINETEEN

THE LARGE VISUAL screen turned off automatically once the after-action log was completed. It might have been the fifth or sixth time Bennett had seen the eight-minute summary of an engagement that had gone on for hours while he and his team were on Mars. Sitting comfortably in an empty large conference room, the same room he'd sat in at the beginning of the mission, he was both happy and conflicted at the same time. With nothing but black battle dress uniform made specifically for covert operations in tropical environments, he was embarrassed that he had a blanket on him, a shawl in essence, as he found the *Robert E. Lee*'s environmental controls too cold at seventy-five degrees Fahrenheit. He felt most comfortable in the engine room, the interior sections where the engines were mounted and running, at a temp well above ninety-two degrees. There, he didn't break a sweat.

He took a deep breath, as if he were about to watch something he knew was terrible but he had to do it anyway. He pushed the button to start with his left hand, then shifted in his seat so that his left eye was more centered on the screen. The room lights dimmed again, and he heard background chatter, ship maneuvering, and periodic bangs, pops, and electrical arcs. The audio and visuals blurred in reverse, and the scene settled on a star field with Captain Taylor's voice calling over comms.

". . . Raleigh, respond. You've been running dark, and you are ninety minutes past check-in. We are approaching your last known location. Please respond."

The next entry was Captain's Taylor's sitrep update. By the time the *Lee* arrived at the *Raliegh*'s last location it was nowhere to be found or seen in any projected orbit. Then the *Virginia*'s comms went from fifteen-minute sitreps to silence. Once that happened, the next steps made sense.

"Rather than doing a search grid for the Raleigh, I am heading directly to the Virginia's last known location. Shortwave radio communique from Lieutenant Virgil Johnson at Alpha outpost, Fort Deadly, reports that Captain Willard Bennett's right hand and right eye was severed from his body by Cassandra Kurtz and her crew. The condition of the captain and Specialist Hall remain unknown. What is clear is that with the captain's hand and eye, combatants can access any shuttle as well as key points on either ship. My fear is that the Raleigh has already been commandeered, and the Virginia is under siege. We are making the best possible speed to intercept."

The next transition showed more of the bridge; there was a deep red hue meaning either an attack or emergency alert. The captain was clearly at the end of giving orders when he turned on his command chair's recorder.

"Load all remaining torpedoes and target the Virginia. Launch shuttles to pursue Raleigh before they get out of our field of vision!"

A series of acknowledgements were sounded off, and there was swift movement of busy crew members in the background.

"Fort Sumter has been given the evacuation alert. The

Virginia is in a steep descent heading on a collision course with the garrison on the surface. I take full responsibility for any life loss, but I must destroy that ship before it completes its suicide run."

His attention was diverted to someone talking to him off-screen.

"I know port torpedo bays were hit; use all starboard torpedoes, and do your best to divert, cripple, or destroy that ship. If it hits anywhere near the garrison, within a three-mile radius, the nuclear explosions will level it."

Next, Taylor shifted his focus briefly on the log screen, then took a computer pad to review and talked for the log record at the same time.

> "Most of Virginia's torpedoes missed us, but three hit our armaments on port, and then went into a deep descent with the obvious intent to destroy the fort. The Raleigh was in full retreat and didn't fire anything, most likely captured, and is the escape ship, in addition to being hijacked."

As he spoke, various visuals were added to confirm his summary points. By far, the most chilling visuals displayed the *Virginia* hurtling toward Mars's surface, the front part of the ship glowing red and yellow as it descended. Seeing a ship of the line being converted into a weapon of mass destruction was disturbing yet startling.

"You know, it doesn't get any better when you watch it multiple times," a voice said behind him. He turned around and saw the captain standing by the room's hatchway. Startled at first, Bennett relaxed, then turned off the recorder, making the big screen turn off, retract, and the conference room lights come on. Behind the captain, Bennett could see that there was a yellow alert. Taylor followed his gaze and explained the reason for increased security as he took a seat just across the table.

"Looks like your boy there, Virgil, got into a scrape with the XO over cussing out another junior officer and saying some derogatory words about Hall. Looks like the LT found some balls of steel down in those caverns," Taylor said.

"Ah, fuck me. What's going to happen to him?" Bennett asked.

"Well, if they find him, it will probably be a court martial. There're enough crew members on board to raise doubt about the cause of the assault, and being underground in a hostile environment on Mars for a week might cause enough trauma to make the young man brittle. And unfortunately for the XO, his actions could be construed as hostile and triggering. I'm sure the doctor will sort out a defendable reason for his errant actions," Taylor said.

Bennett took a moment to think about what the captain said.

"If they find him? He's on a military ship. Where's he going? Bennett thought.

Taylor did not wait for Bennett to comment and went right to his next topic.

"I have to say, I like the eye patch. It does give you a pirate look. The scar on the left balances out the patch," he said.

Bennett gave him a look of surprise, and then he laughed once a smirk emerged on Captain Taylor's face.

Bennett initially brought his right hand up, but then realized that he had a prosthetic hook hand, the one with two slightly curved pincers that Hall suggested, and the doctor was able to 3D print. With such a spectacularly failed mission, he knew that going to Earth would be a death sentence. The need for a prosthetic that was simple, with fewer parts and easy to maintain, was going to be important if he was going to be in a hot, dry cavern for the rest of his days.

"When you put it all together, I do have a certain je ne sais quoi," Bennett said.

But then a cloud of darkness came over him as to what his stolen body parts had done. The visible change from a light exchange to darkness was not lost on Captain Taylor.

"Still, I would prefer to be whole, and I am sick of what they used me for," Bennett said.

"Honestly, I think Kurtz would have found a way to complete her mission, whether it be with your body parts or something else."

"Her mission? If it's to destroy all things patrician, she is on target, but the garrison had young men, patricians just staying put, playing soldier before serving on a ship," Bennett explained.

"Those same young men also laid waste of other Freeports, intimidated, harmed, and killed nonpatrician citizens of Mars. When they were warned of consequences, and nothing came, they did worse things. I guess it's no surprise that they didn't believe the imminent threat from above. They were dubious and egotistical that such an attack could done by 'savages, slaves, and colonists.' Hubris. That's the part that gets me," Taylor said.

"I get that her mission is to destroy, but I can't see anything else," Bennett said.

"Oh, I can. Her coordinated attack, off-planet no less, shows that her reach exceeds well beyond her caverns but also to Freeport, the surface, and even orbit. And to a large degree, she's right: Earth will never be able to win the hearts and minds of these people—Freeport, Kurtz, and even Fort Deadly—because they have constructed a mixed population that works well together, and there is no interest or investment to get back the old ways that are carried over from Earth. Destroying the *Virgina* and Fort Sumter and stealing the *Raleigh* all demonstrate the sheer will to win when pushed, the strength to do that," Taylor said.

Bennett looked carefully at the captain. While he was terribly upset about the loss of life, there was no animosity toward Kurtz and her people for what they did. It was clear that Taylor understood the enemy far better than anyone in the admiralty and Earth.

Suddenly, the dark cloud lifted from the captain's face, and a more positive expression and voice came to life.

"But Captain Bennett, this is not why I came here to see you today," Taylor said.

"Oh? What's the occasion?" Bennett asked.

"To my surprise, the admiralty has sent three other ships that will arrive in seventeen months. I've been ordered to stay on station and 'beat back the mongrels,' even though our food supplies will be out in twelve months," Taylor said.

"Oh," was all Bennett said.

"In addition, the doctor got a brief note from the Fleet Command CMO—for his eyes only—about how to 'prep people in cryo-sleep to ensure that memories can be fully recovered even if deceased.' Can you believe this bullshit?" Taylor explained.

Fuck. It figures, he thought.

"Okay. Well, I guess we're on the chopping block. Captain? If I could, I'd be happy to go into cryo-sleep right now, but could you get Hall off ship? She didn't do anything wrong," Bennett said.

"I have no intention of freezing you and Hall and handing you both over. I might as well jettison you from the ship. Walk with me for a few minutes," Taylor said.

———

The yellow klaxon was still running. The pace was brisk, and that was because the difference in Mars's cavern system, compared to the ship, was nothing less than more than comfortable, even a bit chilly.

"There was part of my communique I have left unread. Before I open it up, I want to make sure you and Specialist Hall are off this ship," Taylor said simply.

Bennett didn't need a crystal ball to see what was going to happen if the captain did what the admiralty ordered—a journey back to Earth, a quick hearing, and sentencing to prison or execution for failing the mission, or worse, being classified as a traitor for complicity,

Still, as dark as it was, Bennett couldn't help but chuckle.

"Yup. I'm surprised you didn't find me a traitor. Was it the severed hand and eye and the time in a convection oven at Fort Deadly? Any of those things gave it away," Bennett said.

"Devious. Devious I say," the captain said.

It took only a few minutes to get to the flight deck. He was not too surprised to see Hall waiting for him, with computer tablet in hand and two larger-than-expected backpacks and carry-ons for what he could see was going to be an extended stay on Mars.

"I hope you don't mind my taking the liberty of packing your bags," she asked.

"Nope. I just hope you took a lot of extra water," Bennett said.

Hall handed Captain Taylor a computer pad. He took it, signed it, and then handed it to Bennett to sign.

"It's your letter of resignation and refusing your commission," Taylor said.

"It's a very patriotic resignation. You explain the guilt and shame of not being killed in battle. Regret that your severed body parts were used to hijack and weaponize a ship, and that you can't think of anything more appropriate than to atone for your failures as to be a full-time resident of Mars, never to show your face again on your beloved home, Earth," Hall recited.

As Hall was telling him about his resignation, six soldiers

with packs like their own walked by them by twos and boarded the waiting transporter. Taylor turned and noted their approach and departure.

"You got everyone, Ellis? Fort Deadly will be happy that you and your engineer volunteers are heading down to help them," Taylor said.

"Me too, sir. I got our five plus one specialist. It was an honor serving with you," Ellis said.

"The honor was mine. Godspeed," Taylor said.

"Thank you, sir."

I'm really going to miss this guy, Bennett thought, and then he looked back at the signature page and signed it.

Another young man appeared, whispered in Taylor's ear, and gave him a clear wrapped package. Taylor looked at it, thanked the young man, and turned to talk to them again with the package held behind his back.

"Well, Captain Taylor, it truly was an honor serving with you," Bennett said.

"Me as well, Captain. I can honestly say I never would have made it without you, the doctor, and the chief. Thank you, sir," Hall said.

Her voice cracked a little on the last part of her goodbye, and then she looked to the ground immediately, as if to not show that her eyes were watering.

"Damn filters. Dust gets everywhere," she said.

"It sure does," Bennett said.

"The honor was mine. Further, this is probably not going to be a forever goodbye as Kurtz is still out there. We will need to trade with Freeport for supplies to stay on station, and who knows what the future will bring? Nonetheless, good luck, citizen Willard Bennett, and thank you for your years of dedication to service and beyond, Specialist Betsy Ann Hall. As you are on Mars, you are a free agent. Still, I hope you raise this flag with honor, and may it flutter to the end of our days," he said, and then handed the package to her.

Hall looked like she was going to say something, but her throat cracked. She did her best to nod, took the package, and stood once again looking down at the flight deck.

"Really, Captain Taylor, you have to do something about those filters," Bennett said.

He then extended his right hand until he realized it was his new hook. The captain grabbed it anyway, shook it, and then walked away.

When he reached the hatch leading out of the flight deck, the doctor and chief engineer were waiting for him. They gave him and Hall a quick wave, and then walked off with Captain Taylor.

———

Bennett grabbed his gear as did Hall. They crossed the deck to get to the transport where an anxious Ellis was waving to them to board faster than they were walking.

Rather than dwelling on or lingering around an emotionally laden situation for Hall, Bennett decided it was his turn to distract her from her pain.

"I don't remember any wind at Fort Deadly, do you?" Bennett asked.

"None, Bennett. But the explosion from the nuclear blast created micro vents to the surface. Lieutenant Strong reports that there have been winds, and it looks like there are some weather events happening way south of the fort's position. When I say *weather events*, it's mostly warm rain, smog, and a stronger smell of sulfur dioxide," Hall said.

"Well . . . that's, ah, promising," Bennett said.

Bennett let Hall get on the transport shuttle first. Once he was aboard, he turned and shut the hatch with a firm thud.

He didn't even see Ellis on his right side, waiting to close the hatch for him.

"Oh, okay. Let me stow your gear," Ellis said.

"No problem. I got it. I'll follow Hall."

Bennett took just a few more steps starboard and dropped his gear with all the rest of the passengers and turned to take a seat.

He took a moment to take stock of an interesting sight; with six available rows up front, all the occupants were taking up the last rows of seats, in the back of the shuttle.

Hall waved him down to join her in the very last row.

"I saved you a seat," she said.

He lumbered down the aisle, and she got up to give him the seat closest to the restroom.

"So, if we are in a near-empty transport shuttle, and there are no patricians to defer the front seats to, why are we in the back row, and the very last seats in the back?" Bennett asked.

Hall gave him a "didn't I tell you this already?" look and continued buckling herself in while balancing her gift, the triangular clear package that clearly enclosed some heavy cloth, on her lap. He was about to ask again when Ellis, the guy who wanted to help him put his gear away, explained.

"Data shows that the structural integrity is much better back here than up there."

Huh? So that explanation is true? I thought that was bullshit for the XO or an excuse for me to use.

"What? That's a thing?" Bennett asked.

"Yes, everyone knows that," Ellis said.

"Then why do the patricians always sit up front?" Bennett said.

"No idea. They always seem to want to sit up front. It's an access thing or to get off the shuttle faster. Never made sense to me," Ellis explained.

Bennett was still thinking when Hall started helping him buckle into his seat.

"Really? You're strapping me in like I'm a child? And you just let people sit up front knowing that if it crashes, they are more likely to die? Fucking ice in your veins, Hall," he said.

After five failed attempts to buckle the left quarter of his body in place, he took a brief rest and debated asking for help.

If Hall was watching, she was doing an excellent job hiding it.

No, I'm going to do this, he thought.

After another three attempts, two that almost made it, he found himself sweating, annoyed, and eventually gave Hall a defeated look. Without missing a beat, she took the strap to finish what he'd started, checked to make sure all contacts were secure, and gave him some advice.

"Okay, it's going to take time to get fine motor control with your right hand, so take it easy and ask for help. You'll practice, and you'll get better. You've survived worse. And people are smart enough to make choices, so if they want to sit up in front and possibly die in a crash, that's their choice. If getting on first and leaving first trumps safety, so be it. I didn't tell them where to sit, even though they would always tell us where to sit," she said.

Bennett remained silent and was annoyed that he had been schooled again. He straightened his expression to make sure he was not pouting. That would have been the final insult.

He looked down at Hall's lap and saw she was fingering the cloth under its transparent covering.

"What did he give you?" he asked.

She seemed startled, immersed in thinking while touching the material.

"Oh, it's an old flag I've always wanted to have. It's a reconstructed MAC–SOG flag with the colors and symbols: the skull with lightning bolts on the sides, wearing a beret, flames for eyeballs, on a red field embedded on a black flag," she said.

"Oh, I remember. I saw it the first day you gave the briefing," Bennett said.

"I have a thing for flags. They have meaning, and they flutter in the wind and let everyone know who you are and what you're all about," Hall added.

Bennett sat still for a moment. He was remembering what Hall had told him about Kurtz "unfurling the black flag," and now here was sitting right next to one.

A blue klaxon flashed in silence, indicating a noncombat flight. Bennett could feel the engines starting, and because he was in the last seat closest to the engine, the vibration was strong.

Ellis turned to offer him a vomit bag, and he declined. He was surprised to see everyone took one but him and Hall. He wondered if harsh sailing was ahead.

"Hey, how come everyone has a toss bag? Are we in for some bad chop?" Bennett asked.

"Probably. The new guy in front warned me about how the atmosphere is thicker than it used to be, and there's often bad chop. I guess the last time he was here, he remembered seeing a guy throw up on himself, and he wasn't going to make the same mistake," Ellis explained.

"What? Who told you that?" Bennett asked.

Ellis looked to the left, then right, of a person blocking his view and pointed out a tall guy, bald under a hat, the only guy wearing a hat, holding a vomit bag at the ready.

"The guy's name is Virgil. I hear he spent a couple of days underground on Mars. Might be bullshit, but he's been more helpful than the usual 'fucking new guy' we usually get," Ellis said.

"Really," Bennett said.

"If half of what he said is true, he's got balls of steel. You know, he likes to hang out with the turbines, deep in the engine room? He's unique," Ellis said.

"Yup. He does seem unique," he replied.

Bennett looked at where he could see the back of the man's head. The attempt to conceal his identity would have worked if Bennett wasn't so familiar to him.

"What's so funny?" Hall said.

"Virgil's on board and is joining us. Seems like old times," Bennett said.

A rare, broad smile appeared on Hall's face, and she looked out her port window.

"Talk about balls of steel. He knows what's down there, and he's willing to abandon his post to get there," she said.

"His days in the service with the XO were limited. You heard he punched him out, right? Kicked a couple of his cronies to the side," Bennett asked.

"I was there. Obviously, loyalty and fair play are important to him," Hall said.

Bennett was still chuckling when the engine reached terminal velocity and launched the craft into open space. He had an image of the XO being a dick and Virgil knocking him on his ass.

That asshole had it coming, he thought.

PART 6

"But you might be more useful as the 'Guardians of the Gates,' the ones that hold the lines against Earth's expansionism and bigotry."

CHAPTER TWENTY

BENNETT LOOKED out to his left and right at the exterior perimeter of Fort Deadly as Ellis was pointing out potential construction sites a mere fifty feet outside the walls. With only a sidearm and Ellis's fully equipped kit in case a canine or feline monster came by, Bennett was feeling calm. He had felt that way since his arrival nearly two years ago, and since he'd discovered that Lieutenant Strong was all about keeping his men safe and secure. That meant opening communications and a bartering system with Freeport and beyond.

Ever since Bennett met Strong and his men, they had been less focused on Earth's politics and caste system, in addition to being abandoned by the admiralty. And while they would assist the admiralty when goals aligned, Strong and his men were all about "we live here and need to get along with our neighbors," whether they be ex-slaves, plebs, surfers, or patricians. There would be no going to war against Freeport or anyone else on behalf of Earth.

Further, when Hall gave Strong her MAC–SOG flag to unfurl and raise above the fort, it did seem like a turning point, a point of no return. First, with the destruction of the garrison, Fort Sumter, the cracks in the surface, from less than an inch to mostly microscopic, had penetrated the crust and reached the cavern. That exposure to the atmosphere allowed for wind, consistent and perpetual movement of hot air. So, for the unfurled black flag, it was fluttering forever in the wind.

Secondly, from a geopolitical perspective, there would be no going to war with Freeport, freed slaves, and plebs, and no going after Kurtz and her people, who were demographically the same as Fort Deadly and Freeport. While there was some bitterness in how Kurtz used him to push Earth back, he still found it hard to hate her for it. He would look at his right prosthetic, feel the eye patch and scar on his cheek, and not feel simmering hate, hot anger, and cold, calculating vengeance, but rather, "I could have been dead, not enjoying these moments."

Bennett had been pondering a long-standing dilemma. While he was sure that if Earth's admiralty attacked Freeport, Strong would not join Earth's attack, would he go to their aid against Earth? So far, Hall, Strong, and himself were still figuring that one out, and the closest to a solution would be that Fort Deadly was amnesty for anyone, a safe harbor within and just outside their walls, albeit fifty feet outside the walls.

"Ah, you with me, sir?" Ellis asked.

Focus, Bennett, he thought.

"Have I told you guys that all you engineers are just crazy? I mean, when you came to me about using reprogramed nanites to thicken the exterior walls, create perimeter bunkers, and to create a sublevel beneath the base's footprint, I said, 'Yeah, sure, you crazy bastards,'" Bennett said.

"And you were pretty freaked out when we got it all done in three months, right?" Ellis said with his usual infectious enthusiasm.

"Yes, yes, I know. And twelve months later, we have more room for everyone who passes through," Bennett said.

"I'm just thinking that you Patties like your quarters indoors and on the surface, and us plebs like it below. I think it's only fair that we create more open space for the surfers and Blacks that come by and stay, since they hate being indoors and behind walls," Ellis said.

"Okay, well not all of us 'Patties' like being indoors, and I've been known to stay outside of my quarters . . ." Bennett started but was cut off before he could fully defend his weak point.

"Like, never. Come on, the LT and a quarter of his guys will stay outside but still inside the wire while Virgil's teams are totally native outside the wall, so they don't count. The women like the aboveground quarters, while the plebs live to keep an eye on you people from below," Ellis said.

Bennett's eyes narrowed as he looked at Ellis.

"I'm joking," he amended, "but most of you guys and the women like being in quarters on the surface, and we have a shit ton of space now below, and the former slaves and surfers are finding places just outside the wire."

Bennett knew that there were some preferences based on prior situations: Freeport's visitors tended to like staying over at Fort Deadly, with half belowdecks and the other half just outside the wire, while all the former slaves, male and female, opted for complete freedom of movement at any point by staying outside the wire, camping, so to speak, under the fort's exterior walls.

Bennett thought Ellis's idea over a year ago was crazy, but it proved to be important. It opened a bridge for trade and commerce to Freeport and anyone who wanted a place to stay in a secure setting before heading off to the frontier. Lieutenant Strong and his men benefited from gear, goods, food, water, alcohol, and companionship. Freeport got fresh canine and newly discovered rat meat, and defensive and survival training for exploring the Martian wild. Nearly all surfers, Blacks, and some plebs really wanted the training. They would come for three weeks to work with Virgil, go off-grid for two months, and come back with maps, stories, and observations. That's how it would go until they left for good.

Where do they go? Bennett had always wondered.

"So, after talking to all the Blacks and surfers, they would much appreciate the twenty outdoor structures outside the wall within fifty feet of the perimeter. Thirty by thirty feet, half covered and the remaining area open, with a drop-down area for a cooking pit and a twelve-foot hole, fifteen feet away, for a latrine. All doable within one month," Ellis said.

"And why are you asking me? I'm not part of the command structure. I've always been a consultant at best here," Bennett said.

"I know, but the LT and Virgil like to have your opinion on things before they let me do anything. Something like an 'elder statesman,' the LT said," Ellis explained.

"Great. Ask the old guy," Bennett said aloud.

Honestly, there was very little need for Ellis to explain as thoroughly as he did what he wanted to do. It was a great idea to use nanites as he proposed, and their past use did nothing but build simple structures that allowed and nearly totally desegregated groups of vastly different people to live and work together. A community vastly different from Earth.

Bennett could see Strong exiting the main gate. He looked around, and when he saw them, started walking toward them. In the cavern's perpetual twilight illuminated by distant reflecting lava rivers and flows, "seeing" was probably less accurate than recognizing the lieutenant's stance, movements, and gait in addition to his approximate height, build, and habits, such as always surveilling the area no matter how short the distance from base command.

"Okay, okay. Honestly, I think it's a great idea, and if

Strong, Hall, and Virgil think it's a good idea, that works for me," Bennett said.

"See? I knew you would agree," Ellis said.

"Whatever he's agreeing to, it probably makes sense," Strong said to them both.

Ellis was a little startled, as his back was in the direction of Strong's approach. He fully recovered once he recognized Strong.

"You could warn me next time," Ellis said, and without further discussion, he walked back to the fort, presumably to get started on the new project.

"He does have good ideas," Strong said.

"He sure does. You know, you all don't have to run things by me. I'm just a civilian, helping," Bennett said.

Strong chuckled and directed Bennett to follow him. Even after years of living in the largest, deepest cavern known to man, it was still hard to think of himself as a cave dweller on a distant planet.

"Yeah, sure, and Hall is *just* a specialist and Virgil is *just* an instructor. Anyway, I was about to tune in to see if our favorite anarchist will be broadcasting today. She's been doing weekly rants at 0100 hours. You heard the last one, right?" Strong asked.

Bennett had been listening to them all for a while on his own transceiver when he was in range. They were vastly different from when he'd first heard them years ago. Over the last fifteen months, they were far less belligerent, less about total anarchy and "fuck Earth," and much more conciliatory, more about being "Martians" and being a blended society.

"Yes," Bennett finally answered.

"Is it me, or has she changed again? Less hostile, more focused on détente, live and let live," Strong commented.

"She sure has," Bennett said.

Through the main gate, beyond the courtyard with sunkin bunkers in case of breach, and just left of the third ammunition store, Strong and Bennett entered one of many nondescript buildings that only those who had been in there would know as the comms room.

There was a large transceiver rig with wires heading down the table legs and out underground to another part of the wall. The room was brighter and warmer due to the power station, battery stores, and two battery-generated lanterns that made the room comparably bright.

Hall was already there with yet another computer pad and her clinical expression, though she did offer a faint smile when she saw them.

"You're late. She started a minute ago, stopped, and now I'm waiting," she said.

"That's been a thing lately too," Strong said. He pointed to a seat for Bennett to sit next to Hall while he pulled up another one.

Just as Bennett sat down, the transceiver came to life. It was difficult to determine if Kurtz had been talking all along or was just picking up where she had left off.

". . . are all Martians now by default. All of us are intrinsically tied to one another by allowing ourselves to be who we are, not who we were cast to be. Slave? No more. Plebs? Gone. Patricians? No longer. Surfers —we are all surfers on Mars . . . Freeport, the frontier, and even Fort Deadly are just the launching points. There is a promised land. We found it. It's real and exists. While Fort Deadly has made more room for their visitors, it never fills to capacity. Freeport has more room every day for new arrivals from the colonies, not less. Where do they all go? Does the frontier eat them up? Are they victims of the badlands? No. The oasis has been found. You will hear more of this as time goes by, but it will be in spurts and whispers. I have known just a handful to have left only as sentries, guards, and couriers devoted to those who want others to live free. What they describe is real. But hear this: Leave your hatreds behind. The angry ones. The resentful ones. The entitled ones—stay away.

"And for our enlightened, older patricians, this place will be hardest for you—it will be most difficult for you to unplug from how you were raised. It will be more difficult for you to be in a truly free society. You can come. On Mars, you are Martian. Live and let live. But you might be more useful as the 'Guardians of the Gates,' the ones that hold the lines against Earth's expansionism and bigotry. You will be the first line of defense against Earth, because Earth is coming. And should you fight, deter, and defend, you will win because of a homefield advantage, resolve, and more people who believe in one people, one place, and one purpose—a free Mars.

"You will also not fight alone. Paradise is not free. We will come when you need us. When you call for us. We are everywhere. We will know when Freeport struggles against Earth. We will know if Fort Deadly is the last stand. We will know when the colonies revolt and join our cause. We will know when to arrive, en masse, in force, for victory or death . . ."

The voice cut out, and static filtered in. Hall attempted to tune in to another frequency to see if there was a chance to get more.

Just like times before, Bennett was entranced by Kurtz's voice. She always had something to say, often something revealing and at times prophetic. Most importantly, her messages were determined, sooner or later, to be accurate.

"I had heard rumors of this place she talks about. And her intelligence is true; for as many people that come through her, come back, and then go off again, never to return, we are always half to three quarters full, never to capacity," Strong said.

"So, as always, she's close, in person or by proxy," Bennett said.

"There could be such a place, an oasis of sorts," Hall said.

Bennett waited for her to go on. When she didn't, he looked at Strong, who also was waiting. It was now common for Hall to say something revealing or important and continue to sit back and ponder her thoughts in silence.

"And this place could exist how?" Strong finally asked.

Hall refocused and returned to where she had left off.

"Oh, yes. Well, the surface fissures from the Sumter blast changed the internal environment of our world. We have perpetual breezes, more humidity, and vegetation has increased in volume and density. And the psychoactive material the big creatures are eating has made them less violent, unless they are hallucinating," Hall explained.

"Yeah, but a 'promised land' of milk and honey?" Bennett asked.

"Well, maybe more of a place of temperate climate—less heat and cooler, less acidity, more alkaline, and purer water. Maybe conifers and flowers, mist, fog, and rain—I mean, we are at the equator, and we know there are large reservoirs of water in the permafrost around the planet, but I would guess there is a lot more, maybe more flowing water, near the poles. We really haven't explored much farther than the cave where we last saw Kurtz. Freeport is all about building their infrastructure, and the colonies have pulled back to their walls. There's just a lot we don't know about this planet," Hall said.

Bennett sat back in his chair to take it all in.

"And she's right about Earth coming back," Strong said.

"Yeah. There is that," Hall said.

"And she knows a lot about what we do here too. And it's not like I can lock down the base. That would alienate everyone, put everyone edge, and my boys would lose their minds without women and leave for Freeport. She's got us there," Strong said.

"The problem with a more open, equitable society," Bennett said.

The room fell silent except for the now barely audible static from the transceiver. It was a comfortable silence, though. The type where good friends or family could sit in one another's company and not feel the need to fill the gap, to be quiet together.

"I think I'll pull together a group of explorers. I'll do a recon to her last location first, get some clues and ideas where to head, but I think it will be one of the poles," Hall said.

"Not a bad idea. Who do you want in the group?" Strong asked.

"Whoever Virgil says is good. More women than men. More ex-slaves, if possible," she said.

"More motivated to find this place? Less of an invading force and more of an expedition? Smart, as always," Bennett said.

"Do you think she's right? The part where she said we, as in Fort Deadly, would be restless in Eden and might be better at keeping the gates free from the admiralty? You know, 'Guardians of the Gate,'" Strong said.

For Bennett, the answer was easy. He had long thought about his changes and redemption.

"Well, for me, I have no great love for Kurtz. First, she took my life when I got back to Earth, and I got jail time. And then I get here and she uses me, or rather, my eye and hand, to kill a lot of patricians. I'm not a fan. But she's right about Earth's faults, and that Earth won't allow everyone to be free. And while I can't stand her, I respect her cause, and I'm not going to let anyone tell me what to think and do, so yeah, I'd keep assholes like Lee from kicking in my door and ordering me to submit. Fuck that shit," Bennett said.

Bennett was surprised by his intensity and conviction. From Hall's and Strong's expressions, they were surprised too.

"Well, then, it's decided—Hall's expedition to the Promised Land is a go. Bennett's Brigade will stand firm with the Guardians at the Gate, and Virgil's Lefties Rangers will prepare for war," Strong announced.

Hall laughed. Her smiles and distractions were more common, but her laughter was a newer development. It wasn't just the laugh, but a laugh that once it got going would be punctuated with snorting. Strong made it his life's goal to get her there. And while her laughing would have normally been enough to distract him, Bennett was trying to figure out the meaning of *Virgil's Lefties Rangers*. He had heard it mentioned before, but when he asked, there would be some lame excuse given, and the subject dropped. It was only when he realized that Virgil was right-handed that he began to think it was more of an inside joke.

"So, seriously, do you think it's nice for Virgil to use my forced amputation to commit a violent act funny? I mean, are you all really okay with him calling his troops *Lefties Rangers*? You're kind of sick fucks, you know that, right?" Bennett said in the best serious voice he could muster.

Hall's laugh increased in volume, and the snorting erupted louder than he could have imagined. Strong was now pointing at her with glee, seeing that she had really lost her shit.

Bennett couldn't help but broadly smile. It was times like this when he would think that if he'd never left Earth, never gone to the Delta Exchange, never saw Kurtz again, moments like these and more life to come never would have occurred. Experiences like these made him happy.

CHAPTER TWENTY-ONE

CASSIE WATCHED Hall from a safe distance. Lying prone between two heating vents throwing more heat around her, in addition to the lava river, she remained still, peering through a small monocular she'd found at Freeport for her great journey. The subject was a mere one hundred feet away. Her usual black compression top and bottom made no noise, but her weapons were the most likely to reflect her location. The heat waves most likely obscured her position, disrupting any image that close to the ground, and she was close enough to talk to Aletheia without being overheard. She could see that Hall was done with the light maintenance on her rifle and was getting herself ready for some kind of rest, an hour of light sleep maybe before she continued her trek. Based on Aletheia's assessment, Hall was heading back to the cave where she had camped to look for clues.

Or to track you so she can kill you? I mean, you have no idea what kind of relationship she has with Bennett, Aletheia said.

"Weren't you the one that figured out that Bennett had changed? He really can't return to Earth and is stuck here? How he wasn't even interested in killing me, and that he was just done with all the bullshit," Cassie said.

Yes, but she's a mix of class, and maybe she hates one over the other? Conflicted or something. I don't know, but maybe she has allegiance to Bennett or his bosses and will try to kill you as you sleep one night, Aletheia said.

"Maybe, but I doubt it."

There was silence in her head for a moment. She continued watching Hall checking on her perimeter warnings, which were more than usual. She was out in the open, close to the lava river and heat vents to keep most of the creatures away, but not everything, especially humans. Cassie also took a closer look at her prosthetic left knee when she walked around, her short hair length, how she moved her hands, transitioned from fine motor control to gross motor, and transitioned back. Cassie found her spirit, intelligence, and tenacity attractive.

Or you could be a dumbass in love with her, or just lust, Aletheia said.

"Okay! How would you know that unless you were able to dig into my mind? If we weren't friends and you weren't hardwired into my brain, we'd be having a serious discussion about removing you from me to a computer chip," Cassie said.

I fucking knew it! What has she seen in my head? Cassie thought

Aletheia continued. *Really? You think I had to read your mind to figure this out? The doctor called it when he saw you interact with her at the cave. Now what was it?* . . . "*Your attention seemed divided between the captain and the specialist,*" *he said.*

Cassie remained quiet. She had to give her that one.

And then, the first thing out of your mouth to Gavin, Nancy, and recon after two years of searching, finding, and coming back with the map to get there was your interaction with— again, pointed out by the doctor—"Specialist Hall and the captain," Aletheia added.

Yeah. That was stupid obvious, Cassie thought.

And since you have no interest in men, and even if you did, you would be hard-pressed to be with one of your tribes, which I do not understand . . .

"Okay, Aletheia. You're right. Okay? You win. So, can we get back to work here?" Cassie said.

Aletheia stopped talking in her head for a moment. In lieu of that, her image appeared on Cassie's optic nerve. She hadn't changed much except to have shortened hair in braids, less clothing like Cassie, as if she felt the heat the way everyone else did and the same assortment of edged weapons minus firearms.

You see. The truth will set you free, she finally said.

Cassie continued her surveillance and scanned potential approach vectors.

And when you say, "work," the only thing I'm seeing is stalking. And since I really can't read your mind, and we've established you like her at least and are attracted to her, can you tell me the plan? Why are you here, and what do you want to do? Aletheia asked.

Cassie put her monocular down, placed her hands under her chin for support, and took time to really figure out what she wanted to do. Aletheia, modelled from an early twenty-first century human psychologist, waited and allowed the process to continue uninterrupted.

Minutes went by as she continued to think. After much mental gymnastics, internal discussions, past and present, intellectual posits and counterarguments, Cassie felt as if she could answer the question. She remained in her same position, though she still scanned her area and Hall as she napped.

"This is all a guess, but I think Hall and I are similar. She's not a patrician but not a pleb or surfer either. She's clearly capable of living out here in the wild, but she must have been able to manage the political blood sport on a ship to get here, and clearly earned the admiration of patrician men, which is next to impossible to do. I think she's capable of fitting in but is out here instead. She communicates back to their fort and others in the field, but it's not a sitrep, more social. I wonder if she's tired of all things people and Earth, and if she would want to have an adventure with someone who kind of gets her, and not be lonely in being free," Cassie said.

As Cassie spoke, Aletheia's image remained still, except for her nodding for her to continue.

"Honestly, I'm lonely, and I'd like to go to our new place with someone whom I could get to know better, and who might be like-minded," Cassie said.

Aletheia was still, as if thinking, and then nodded before she spoke.

You might be right. And what I am hearing is that you are lonely, and you think she is too, and you would like her to come with you. It really makes sense. I mean, it's a big ask. You're asking her to drop everything to go with you, Earth's greatest terrorist, on a seven-month journey, to a newly discovered, never-before-seen land, Alethea said.

"Not just any land, but a land of conifers, small oceans of fresh water, cool climates where you need fire to get warm, corn, unbelievably, and plenty of wildlife for hunting. The actual Promised Land," Cassie said.

All true, almost too true. Let's hope she believes you, Aletheia said.

"So, if she were to leave her radio behind, and since we are four months behind everyone, there's no risk of exposing the main group," Cassie added.

And the sentries along the route will help; yes, it's all good if she comes. And finding such a place on this world, no one in their right mind would want to leave, Aletheia said.

The conversation stopped for a moment.

So, what are you waiting for? You already know she's alone. You've seen her trip wires, and it won't take much for you to disarm her before she even knows you're there, Aletheia said.

There was more silence. Cassie continued to survey the area, marking out her approach, and already knew how she would disarm her. But there was a big thing getting in her way. She was thinking about how she would explain it to Aletheia without sounding juvenile, an immature teenager.

Cassie? Are you still with me here? Aletheia said.

"I don't know if she would even like me," Cassie blurted out.

Aletheia's image froze for a moment, and then her jaw slackened, and a smile emerged.

Ah, come on! Don't be a dumbass, Cassie thought.

Aletheia smile was small. To her credit, she did not berate or embarrass Cassie but gave her advice that she was sure a nonpatrician therapist would have given more than a hundred years ago.

Cassie, it makes sense. I'm not going to be an asshole here. I'm just going to say this—you had an abbreviated childhood, no teen stuff, no young adult stuff like friends, intimate and otherwise, and then, due to your convictions of equality and fair play, you're a terrorist put in prison, then sent to Mars, almost enslaved into marriage, and then you become a leader for all nonpatricians on the planet. No time to have a moment or two for what might pass as a 'normal' private life. So, here's the deal. If you don't ask, you won't know, and she won't know, Aletheia said.

Cassie remained still and took her time to process all that Aletheia had said. It was a lot. It was important.

"I suppose the great Cassandra Kurtz really has been too busy to have a social life," Cassie finally said.

Absolutely. So, tell her exactly what you told me about wanting her to come along. It's genuine, truthful, no bullshit, and she will be impressed with the honesty and how you're seemingly at ease with yourself, your power, and your person, Aletheia coached.

"Yeah. I should be able to do this," Cassie said.

She looked through her glass again and could see that Hall was not looking in her direction. She got up into a crouch to head left of her position. She stowed her monocular away to free up her hands when she moved.

Unless she laughs at you and thinks you're an entitled egotist to think she would drop everything for you. Kind of ballsy, you know, Aletheia added.

Cassie dropped to the ground again, as if she were dodging a sniper round that was zeroing on her head. She was back in her prone position with her head lying face down in her hands.

"Fuck! I'm out. Stupid, stupid, stupid," Cassie blurted out.

I'm just messing with you, Cassie. You can do this. You've taken on the patriarch, racists, and a self-entitled caste system; freed slaves, surfers, and plebs; and you've shown them a new way to live—free to live where and how you want, love who you want, and to be your genuine self on a new planet. I think you can ask another person to join you on a new quest, Aletheia said.

Logically, Cassie knew that Aletheia was right, but she still lay face down, not moving.

Honestly, after what you've been through, don't you think you're entitled to a little happiness? she said.

Cassie let a little more time pass before she looked up, pulled herself together, pushed adolescent embarrassment aside, and stood up straight at first, then moved like she had a purpose.

Okay. We're doing this. So, when she's looking at you, stand straight, don't slouch, and keep eye contact as you talk. Don't be afraid to push your boobs out just a little more if you could . . . Aletheia said.

"Okay, if I'm doing this, I can't have you in my head. It will be too distracting," Cassie.

No problem. We'll do an after-action report when she's asleep, Aletheia said.

While Aletheia's choice for gossiping was a bit more militaristic than social, Cassie let it go.

"To the great journey," Cassie said.

To the Promised Land, Aletheia said.

EPILOGUE

EXECUTIVE OFFICER ROBERT LEE VI reviewed his most recent communique from naval intelligence and his updated orders from the admiralty from a secured station far from his office and from the sight of crew members. Escaping prying eyes was far easier these days, once a quarter of the crew abandoned their posts to live on Mars and the captain did nothing to keep it from happening. This laissez-faire management style drove him crazy.

He had been waiting for this moment for a long time, and finally, it had arrived. After months of encrypted reports of Captain Taylor's trading with Freeport, and not being aggressive in finding the hijacked *Raleigh*, and still no efforts to retake Bennett and kill Kurtz, the orders finally came in after close to two years. They were short and to the point:

> Earth Admiralty and Tribunal Command confirm recent orders for Captain Taylor of the Robert E. Lee to initiate aggressive steps to find and secure the Raleigh, refit it for return to service, regroup with the task force in search of Cassandra Kurtz, and support defending the colonies. If he does not comply with these orders within seven solar days of receipt of this dispatch, you are authorized to take command of the Lee and carry out his duties. You will have latitude as to who will need to be detained should there be resistance. Success of this mission and key points will result in field promotion to captain and significant increase in pay and benefits.

XO Lee noted the time stamp was three solar days ago leaving the captain four days left to comply with the admiralty's orders. If not, he could seize command, and his birthright to *Robert E. Lee* would be attained, finally. He couldn't help but smile. He had acknowledged receipt of his orders with zeal, and he had been struggling with trying to keep his emotions in check, especially when giving sitreps and attending status meetings. Before these recent orders, he had been thinking about returning to Earth and calling it a career. He couldn't stomach dealing with such a passive captain and his weak-ass command team.

He reread the document, almost to ensure he was not imagining it. After another read, he folded it, put it in his uniform's inside pocket, stood up, and left the sequestered room with a firm gait, chest out and chin high.

Things are about to change around here, he thought.

He felt the corners of his mouth lift. It had been a very long time since he'd felt a smile on his face.

THE END

ABOUT THE AUTHOR

J.M. Erickson earned his bachelor's degree from Boston College, majoring in psychology and sociology, a master's degree from Simmons University, School of Social Work, and completed post-graduate certification programs in assessment and treatment of psychological trauma and human services management at Boston University.

Erickson continues to work as a high school counselor and community therapist in Merrimack Valley, Massachusetts, USA.

Links

Website – www.jmericksonindiewriter.com
Website – www.jmericksonindiewriter.net
Blog – www.jmeindieblog.com
Kirkus Review –
https://www.kirkusreviews.com/author/jm-erickson/
Amazon – amazon.com/author/jmerickson

ENDLESS FALL OF NIGHT
SAMPLE CHAPTER

Chapter Eleven

"So? Can you see me or not?" Aletheia asked.

Cassie was still processing what she was seeing in her mind's eye. In only one week, Aletheia and Cassie's symbiotic relationship was back to normal, if there were such a thing. In fact, it was better than it had ever been. Just as Aletheia learned about everything that had transpired when she was encrypted and disconnected for two years, kind of her own imprisonment, Cassie learned that Aletheia had an image. No longer a disembodied voice but an actual visage, some of which she previewed when she first came out of her shock last week in sick bay.

"I mean, the peripheral shock not only started me up like a defibrillator, it really charged the nanobots to expand rapidly to other parts of your brain. Cool, huh?" Aletheia said.

Cassie nodded.

In Aletheia's wisdom, she not only downloaded all her knowledge accrued during their ten years together, with corresponding evolution and experience, but a whole lot of data she hacked into, mostly bank and financial records, public criminal information, and private educational institutions' student data. All encapsulated and locked in a massive drive and with a reactivation code that had no radiofrequency locater. Aletheia was fully rogue, enmeshed via nanobots in her brain tissue throughout her head, no longer located in one place. Even if they were to take out the original capsule Aletheia was first in, it would be a mere shell, and Aletheia would continue. She had one weakness: she would die if Cassie died. The good news was that Aletheia, now having access to areas like the occipital lobes, could draw upon Cassie's senses to "show" her things. Aletheia could also help her with movements now, with access to the motor cortex, or assist with abstract thinking in the frontal cortex and dig up locked-away memories and emotions from the limbic system. Cassie wasn't too crazy about the memories, but Aletheia assured her she would not just "take over" or scrutinize an area without Cassie's permission.

But now, seemingly "standing" before her was the image, the way Aletheia saw herself. It was a surprise, even though it shouldn't have been. Cassie had always thought her AI would look like herself, or other women named Aletheia— fair white skin and flawless complexion, with shiny, silky hair. Soft, supple curves; thin but not emaciated; and delicate hands, feet, and fingers.

Her Aletheia, her true sister merged best friend, was nothing like that. First, her skin was a dark mahogany hue. Similarly flawless, though a small mole on her forearm was visible. It did not detract from her strong beauty. Her hair was black, magnificently thick, and curly. She had an athletic build—she reminded Cassie of a male sprinter—and still, you could see how Aletheia's cable-like arms could pose a threat to someone if she was physically present. But it was her young face—the same age as Cassie, but so different—that was captivating. She had big brown eyes, a thin nose at the top that fleshed out toward her mouth, and lips fuller than Cassie had ever seen on another woman. Her lashes were thick and long; her ears were adorned with dangling earrings; and she had multicolored long, manicured nails. She was a cacophony of color, beautifully arranged, full of life. She was truly something Cassie had never seen before.

"So? What's the look for? You look like, I don't know, disturbed or baffled or both," Aletheia said.

Cassie smiled and took her time. She couldn't explain as fully as she wanted due to surveillance, and since she was not doing her log entry, she improvised by opening the lavatory and looking in the mirror. She talked to the mirror as if speaking to her reflection.

"Beautiful. Textured and layered with color. I am so glad it's you," Cassie said quietly.

Aletheia's response was hesitant but clear. *"You are too kind. I have you to thank, though."*

Cassie knitted her eyes and was curious how she could have been remotely involved in such a creation.

"All that data from past servers you bought and gigabits of data and images were at my disposal. I found this image, a famous female doctor of philosophy and practitioner, well versed and heavily cited on forming blended cultures, mixed-race and multilayered identities. Her work predates 2041, but she became a formative voice for what our society would call 'savages.' I really liked the visage."

"Me too," Cassie said.

"And she was an accomplished athlete in running and, believe it or not, kendo, the use of edged weapons. Apparently, her father insisted on her learning. Pretty wild, huh?"

With that last statement, Aletheia's hands moved from her hips to the small of her back to produce two curved blades, and she switched into an obvious fighting pose. It was just amazing. It was like finding your best friend idealized, with enhanced skills and powers, all without jealousy.

"Just perfect," Cassie said.

Cassie remained quiet for a moment, staring at the reflected image looking back. Prison, court, the hateful looks her peers would give, and those frightened looks patricians below her would give, all were weighing on her. She felt she had grown, hardened, become more independent.

Cassie continued looking in the mirror. She took stock of her body. There were some muscles, clearly some scars, and she was thin. Her deep-blue eyes were a bit brighter but far paler, lacking the light and spirit that she would like. She took another moment and looked at Aletheia again, then stood back to take in her entire body. All this time, she had been reacting. Now she thought she would be doing something different, more planful, with an element of surprise, a zig instead of a zag.

Of all the bodily changes, she knew her shaved head, the lack of femininity, and lack of adherence to female "patrician beauty" standards among a ship of men were most disturbing to the officers and crew. Not the plebs. They knew a protest when they saw it.

"You know what, reflection on the wall? I think I want to be the image in my mind's eye. Eight months on this trip? I think I should be in great shape, skilled in survival and weapons. Yes, time to be on the move, planful, and ready. I think it's time to burn the whole fucking thing to the ground," Cassie said.

Aletheia, not one to pause or wait for more information, didn't respond quickly at all. Cassie's verbal plan just hung in the air, until her AI asked the obvious questions.

"OK. So, just so I'm aware, what does that mean?" Aletheia asked. *"Mutiny? Sabotage? Crash the ship?"* she added.

"No. I mean disrupt the patriarchy, free slaves, stir up plebs and surfers, teach the truth, create a rebellion, create havoc and mayhem, and free the colonies from Earth. You know, shake things up a bit," Cassie said.

There was a pause, and then Aletheia smiled, hands akimbo and looking relaxed.

"You know, that's a lot on the docket, but I can help."

———

Available for purchase on Amazon